Read 3-7

BEH 12-7-95

BW

"WHO THE HELL ARE YOU?"

"That's none of your concern, Fargo," she answered.

"Hell, it isn't," Fargo growled. "I'm shanghaied, dragged here, and told to climb into your bed. I want some answers."

"No answers. All you have to do is perform."

"Why me?"

"Why do people hire you to ride trail?" she asked.

"Because I'm the best and they know it."

"Same for this."

Fargo allowed her a slow smile. "Now that's real flattering, but I don't believe you."

"Then believe this. You don't walk out of here alive unless I let you. Are you ready to get on with it now?"

Fargo felt his fury turning to angry desire. "I'm ready," he growled. "And you'd better be." He reached out, grabbed the drawstring of her dress, and pulled her forward as the dress fell to the ground . . .

SIGNET Westerns You'll Enjoy

☐ **THE TRAILSMAN #1: SEVEN WAGONS WEST by Jon Sharpe.**
(#AE1052—$2.25)*
☐ **THE TRAILSMAN #2: THE HANGING TRAIL by Jon Sharpe.**
(#AE1053—$2.25)*
☐ **THE TRAILSMAN #3: MOUNTAIN MAN KILL by Jon Sharpe.**
(#E9353—$1.75)*
☐ **THE TRAILSMAN #4. THE SUNDOWN SEARCHERS by Jon Sharpe.**
(#E9533—$1.75)*
☐ **THE TRAILSMAN #5: THE RIVER RAIDERS by Jon Sharpe.**
(#AE1199—$2.25)*
☐ **THE ANGRY HORSEMEN by Lewis B. Patten.** (#E9309—$1.75)
☐ **PURSUIT by Lewis B. Patten.** (#E9209—$1.75)
☐ **SIGNET DOUBLE WESTERN—LAWMAN FOR SLAUGHTER VALLEY by Ray Hogan and PASSAGE TO DODGE CITY by Ray Hogan.**
(#J9173—$1.95)*
☐ **SIGNET DOUBLE WESTERN—BRANDON'S POSSE by Ray Hogan and THE HELL MERCHANT by Ray Hogan.**
(#J8857—$1.95)*
☐ **THE RAPTORS by Ray Hogan.** (#E9124—$1.75)
☐ **THE DEAD GUN by Ray Hogan.** (#E9026—$1.75)
☐ **SIGNET DOUBLE WESTERN—PATCHSADDLE DRIVE by Cliff Farrell and SHOOTOUT AT SIOUX WELLS by Cliff Farrell.**
(#J9258—$1.95)*
☐ **SIGNET DOUBLE WESTERN—APACHE HOSTAGE by Lewis B. Patten and LAW OF THE GUN by Lewis B. Patten.**
(#J9420—$1.95)
☐ **SIGNET DOUBLE WESTERN—SADDLE AND RIDE by Ernest Haycox and THE FEUDISTS by Ernest Haycox.**
(#J9467—$1.95)
☐ **SIGNET DOUBLE WESTERN—RIM OF THE DESERT by Ernest Haycox and DEAD MAN RANGE by Ernest Haycox.**
(#J9210—$1.95)

*Price slightly higher in Canada

Buy them at your local bookstore or use this convenient coupon for ordering.
THE NEW AMERICAN LIBRARY, INC.,
P.O. Box 999, Bergenfield, New Jersey 07621
Please send me the books I have checked above. I am enclosing $_____
(please add $1.00 to this order to cover postage and handling). Send check or money order—no cash or C.O.D.'s. Prices and numbers are subject to change without notice.

Name_____

Address_____

City _____ State _____ Zip Code _____

Allow 4-6 weeks for delivery.
This offer is subject to withdrawal without notice.

THE TRAILSMAN 11

MONTANA MAIDEN

by
Jon Sharpe

A SIGNET BOOK
NEW AMERICAN LIBRARY
TIMES MIRROR

PUBLISHER'S NOTE

This novel is a work of fiction. Names, characters, places, and
incidents are either the product of the author's imagination
or are used fictitiously, and any resemblance to actual persons,
living or dead, events, or locales is entirely coincidental.

NAL BOOKS ARE AVAILABLE AT QUANTITY DISCOUNTS
WHEN USED TO PROMOTE PRODUCTS OR SERVICES. FOR
INFORMATION PLEASE WRITE TO PREMIUM MARKETING DIVISION,
THE NEW AMERICAN LIBRARY, INC., 1633 BROADWAY,
NEW YORK, NEW YORK 10019.

Copyright © 1982 by Jon Sharpe

The first chapter of this book appeared in *Slave Hunter*,
the tenth volume of this series.

All rights reserved

SIGNET TRADEMARK REG. U.S. PAT. OFF. AND FOREIGN COUNTRIES
REGISTERED TRADEMARK—MARCA REGISTRADA
HECHO EN CHICAGO, U.S.A.

SIGNET, SIGNET CLASSICS, MENTOR, PLUME, MERIDIAN AND NAL
BOOKS are published by The New American Library, Inc.,
1633 Broadway, New York, New York 10019

First Printing, July, 1982

1 2 3 4 5 6 7 8 9

PRINTED IN THE UNITED STATES OF AMERICA

The Trailsman

Beginnings . . . they bend the tree and they mark the man. Skye Fargo was born when he was eighteen. Terror was his midwife, vengeance his first cry. Killing spawned Skye Fargo, ruthless, cold-blooded murder. Out of the acrid smoke of gunpowder still hanging in the air, he rose, cried out a promise never forgotten.

The Trailsman, they began to call him, all across the West: searcher, scout, hunter, the man who could see where others only looked, his skills for hire but not his soul, the man who lived each day to the fullest, yet trailed each tomorrow. Skye Fargo, the Trailsman, the seeker who could take the wildness of a land and the wanting of a woman and make them his own.

The high plains country called Montana,
not yet a territory of its own,
a wild land where men made their
own rules to live by
—or die by.

1

"You want to tell me what the hell this is all about?"

Skye Fargo asked the question as, his hands bound behind him, he took in the four heavy-barreled guns leveled at him. He let his eyes go to the four men behind the guns, their stubbled faces made of grim hardness. The one directly in front of him, a short man with a broad, aggressive face, answered impatiently.

"I told you, it's about screwing," he said.

Instantly Fargo's mind flew backward, searching the past as he stared in disbelief at the man. "Hell, I can't think of anybody who'd be this mad," he murmured.

"Not anything you did," the man said. "What you're gonna do."

The frown dug deeper into Fargo's brow. "What the hell does that mean?" he barked as he twisted his wrist bonds, found them well-tied.

"It means we're getting real good pay to bring you someplace," the man said.

"Someplace where?" Fargo asked.

"Someplace where you're going to screw," the man answered.

Fargo's stare was one of continued disbelief.

1

"Why the goddamn guns? Why not just ask?" he pressed.

"Because you either screw this girl or you don't walk away alive," the man barked.

Fargo's nonplussed stare stayed on the man as only one thought spiraled in his mind and he gave it voice. "This must be the ugliest goddamn girl west of the Mississippi," he murmured.

"I don't know, I never met her." The man shrugged, turned to one of the others. "Get his horse. We've got to get moving," he ordered.

Fargo leaned against the wall of what was clearly a small shack somewhere as one of the men left. The frown stayed deep on his forehead as he let his thoughts go back over the past twenty-four hours. He'd been set up, that much was all too clear, hand-picked before he'd walked into the dance hall, perhaps before he'd even arrived here in Wheeltown. He held the thought for a moment, set it aside. He'd start at the beginning when he'd arrived in Wheeltown yesterday morning.

He'd ridden trail for three Conestogas carrying all the worldly goods of a very large family who hoped they could build a new life here where the Yellowstone and Bighorn rivers joined. They had an uncle waiting for them here, only it turned out that the uncle had caught six Sioux arrows two months ago and he was only a name on a crude wooden cross now. Maybe dreamers and fools were always one and the same, Fargo recalled thinking. It was the kids he felt sorry for, their young lives laid out for the taking by those with more hope than sense. Of all the untamed places, the Montana country was it, made for only the very strong or the very lucky. But the thoughts were his and he took them along with him with his pay and went to find Harry McAteer.

Harry had a tanner's shop in Wheeltown and

Fargo had written him nearly two months back telling him he'd be rolling in one day. Fargo recalled how Harry had exploded in his roaring way when he'd walked into the shop. It had been years since they had ridden trail together and it was a time for remembering, for celebrating, a time for strong bourbon and weak women, and the dance hall had supplied both.

Fargo thought back of how he'd made a note to remember the name of the place, the White Squaw Saloon, and now he had another reason to remember it. Harry had given up a little after midnight, and telling the girl to wait, Fargo helped him to his room over the little tanning shop, dropped him onto the bed, and returned to the saloon. The girl was there, waiting, and he remembered her clearly despite all the bourbon. Edna, not the usual name for a dance-hall girl, and she wasn't the usual type, either, a washed-out blonde with a long, thin figure and smallish breasts that hardly peeked over the low neckline of the dress. But she had good legs, long and willow-wand smooth, and she'd had a distinctive, tinkly little-girl voice that made her easy to listen to and she fitted comfortably into all the remembering he and Harry had done. She'd seen to it that their glasses were quickly filled, but hell, that was part of her job.

Thinking back, frowning at the effort, Fargo remembered how her eyes had seemed terribly wide when he returned, almost frightened. "Let's have one more and then go upstairs," she had said.

Fargo had quickly agreed and she'd fetched the two bourbons, set his before him. She was looking more attractive, he remembered, the long legs suddenly very desirable. He finished his drink in three quick draws and she led him upstairs to a big room with a big bed and very little else in it. She closed

3

the door as he sank down on the bed, looked up at her. Again, her eyes seemed terribly round and uncertain. She'd put her hand to the top of her dress, fiddled with the snaps below the neckline.

"You all right, Edna?" Fargo remembered asking. She nodded as the top of the dress came open and he caught a glimpse of the smallish breasts, remembered thinking how they matched her tinkly little-girl voice. He recalled how he'd started to rise up on his elbows on the bed when suddenly Edna became a blur, a fuzzy, shapeless form. He shook his head and she came into focus again. "Too damn much bourbon," he'd muttered. He half-rose and the room started to spin. He shook his head again and the room straightened out. He stared at Edna and fright was unmistakable in her eyes.

"What's eating you?" He frowned, got to his feet, and suddenly he seemed to have no legs, fell back onto the bed. Edna's figure became a blur again and he shook his head back and forth like a terrier shaking water from itself. She came back into focus and he stared at her. "Goddamn," he'd muttered. "That last drink. You put something in it."

She only stared back at him and he saw the door fly open, the four men rush into the room. He rose and the room began spinning away again, but he brought up a swinging blow that cleared his head as he felt it land on the nearest jaw. He had the satisfaction of seeing the figure fly backward before the scene faded away as a gray curtain dropped over his eyes. He remembered reaching for his gun, his hand moving down, touching the handle of the big Colt. He was doing everything in slow motion, the curtain in front of him now a purple gray. He'd felt hands seizing him, remembered bringing up a tremendous uppercut, somehow with enough force in it to cause a shouted oath of pain.

4

The blow jarred his arm and head and the curtain parted for a moment. The men were coming at him, all except one who was on one knee. "Son of a bitch," Fargo heard one say. As the purple-gray curtain began to slip over him again, he threw another blow, his powerful shoulder muscles fully behind it, and he heard the sound of a figure falling. Head down, he pumped blows, swinging wildly, the purple-gray curtain closing off all vision.

Someone landed atop his back and he felt himself falling forward. His arm struck something, a leg, and he wrapped his arms around it, pulled and twisted, heard the shout of pain, and then hands were yanking him away, rolling him over. He felt hardness, the floor, and what must have been a knee slamming into his back. The purple-gray curtain became thicker, heavier, drifted into blackness. He heard a voice before he passed out, as if from a very far distance.

"Jesus, I'd hate to tangle with him when he's all himself," the voice said, and then the blackness had enveloped him and the world disappeared.

Fargo lifted his glance as the men returned to the little shack, his remembering over for the moment. "I've got the horses," the man said.

"Let's go," the short one with the broad, aggressive face said, and Fargo was led from the shack. He blinked at the bright sunlight, took a moment to adjust his eyes, and saw the pinto waiting. He was helped into the saddle, murmured a few soft words to the pinto, and watched the horse shake its head in greeting. "Helluva good-looking horse, that Ovaro," the broad-faced man said. He let a small hard grin touch his lips. "Easy to spot, too," he added.

Fargo notched the remark in his mind. It fitted.

5

He'd been picked. They'd known about him, how to find him easily. The four men started to ride, two in front, one on each side of him, one holding the reins of the pinto. Fargo tried the wrist ropes again, tightened his hand muscles, but the ropes stayed secure, no give at all in the knots. He let his eyes scan the terrain. It was lush, fertile land, this Montana country, as full of beauty as danger, a wild land of mountain and valley, high plain and heavy tree cover. He glanced back at the little shack where they'd taken him from the saloon. It sat in a clearing, a thin pathway leading south from the door, through a thick stand of hawthorns, and he imprinted the terrain in his mind.

The men moved downward into a shallow valley, through country heavy with oak and hawthorn, birch, elm, and blue spruce, the thick bromegrass soft as a feather pillow underfoot. They rode into the afternoon with only an occasional exchange of words between the four men and finally the broad-faced one called a halt, reached into his pocket, and fished out a crude trail map. He studied it for a moment, pulled his horse to the left. "This way," he muttered, started down a slow slope.

"This sure as hell makes no damn sense," Fargo remarked, blurting out the words angrily. "Why me?" he thrust out.

The man peered at him, shrugged. "Beats me," he said. "Maybe you've got something nobody else has."

"That all you're going to say?" Fargo pushed at him.

"I told you, we're just hired to bring you along," the man said.

"Who hired you?" Fargo asked.

"A friend of hers," the man said.

Fargo lapsed into silence and the frown touched

6

his forehead again. It just didn't make sense. A girl who needed or wanted that bad could get it without any trouble, even an ugly one. Unless she was so damn ugly that nobody'd touch her. Fargo made a face. It was possible, but it somehow didn't set right. Hell, no woman was that ugly. At least, he hoped not. The other question circled again. Why him? Why not someone else? He half-smiled, allowed himself a wry thought. He had something of a reputation and he'd never had an unsatisfied customer, but he wasn't conceited enough to accept that answer. He was still wrestling with the question when the house came into view, a small frame structure. The riders broke into a canter and Fargo felt his mouth tighten. He'd have at least one answer damn soon.

They reined up outside the house, the few windows with drawn curtains, the place silent. A man beckoned to Fargo and the Trailsman swung one leg over the saddle horn, slid to the ground. The broad-faced man took him by the arm, led him to the closed door, and knocked hard three times.

"He's here," the man called out. There was no answer, no sound from inside the house, and Fargo frowned at the closed door. He was staring at it when it slowly swung open by itself. A room, made dim by the drawn curtains, came into view beyond the partly open door. "Inside," the broad-faced man said, helped him with a push in the small of his back. Fargo stepped into the room and the man drew the door closed behind him. The Trailsman's eyes moved around the sparsely furnished room, a few chairs and a table, nothing more, and then he heard the sound, soft footsteps. His eyes went to the doorway of an adjoining room.

His hands behind his back, Fargo stepped forward, stared at the doorway. The figure came into view and Fargo found himself staring at one of the most beautiful girls he had ever seen.

"I'll be damned," he swore softly.

2

The girl stood silently, unmoving, taking in the big black-haired man, his lean, intensely handsome face, the lake-blue eyes that still held astonishment. She moved around the tall figure and Fargo felt her working on the wrist bonds until his hands came loose. He drew them in front of himself as he rubbed circulation back, watched her step back in his view. His eyes moved over the long, thick black hair that hung loose and full far below her shoulders. Black, thin eyebrows arched over eyes, which were pools of black liquid, a straight, patrician nose with thin nostrils and finely etched lips, all contrasting starkly against milk-white skin. His eyes moved down to follow the line of a long, graceful neck that flowed into wide shoulders. She wore a long dress that hung straight yet couldn't hide the soft rise of deep, full breasts and the long curve of her hips. It was tied loosely at the neck with a long drawstring.

"Who the hell are you?" Fargo asked.

"That's none of your concern," she answered, and her voice was low, a husky sound.

"Hell it isn't," Fargo growled. "I'm shanghaied, dragged here, and given orders. I want some answers."

"No answers," she said. "All you have to do is perform."

"You're asking a lot," he said.

"I'm giving a lot," she said.

"That's all your choice, honey," Fargo snapped back. "You can call it off."

The black, liquid eyes met the harshness of his stare and she shook her head, the long jet locks swinging gracefully. "No," she almost whispered.

"Then I want some answers. Why me?" he asked.

"You were handy," she said.

"Bullshit," he threw back at her. "Why me?"

"Why do people hire you to ride trail?" she asked.

"Because I'm the best and they know it," Fargo said.

"Same for this," she said.

Fargo allowed her a slow smile. "Now, that's real flattering," he said, and then, his voice hardening, "But I don't believe a goddamn word of it."

"I don't care whether you do or not," she said sharply, and turned, walked into the adjoining room. "In here," she called, and he followed her. The room was wide, dim, with the window thickly curtained. A large bed and a splintered dresser were the only pieces of furniture. She turned and he tried to read the dark depths of her eyes but gave up quickly. "Let's get done with it," she said, and he caught the hint of a tremor in the husky, low voice. He watched the way her hands clenched and unclenched, the lovely lips drawing thin. Under the contained exterior she was a bushel of held-in, churning emotions.

"Let's talk some more, first," Fargo said.

"No more talk," she said impatiently, "The men who brought you here gave you the terms."

"I don't like them," he said. "Not without more answers."

10

She shook her head and the long black hair swung gracefully. "No more answers," she said.

He eyed her again, tried a different tack. "You've got a name," he said.

She shook her head again. "No names," she said.

"Even a whore has a name," Fargo tossed back, and saw the black, liquid eyes stir, a flash of dark fire. Her lovely face turned away and she thought for a moment.

"Lisa," she said, looking back at him. No lie, he knew at once, no name pulled out of thin air for him. There'd been too much pride in the way she'd said it, her chin lifting almost defiantly.

"Lisa," he echoed, slowly turning the name on his lips. "Lovely Lisa. It fits you."

"Whether you approve or not isn't important," she said with sudden tartness.

"It is to me," he answered, and seemed to take another moment to study her lush beauty. Suddenly, with the speed of a cougar's strike, his hand shot out, caught the top of the dress, and yanked her forward. He saw fright leap into her black eyes. "I want answers, dammit," he growled.

"Let go of me," she said, anger replacing fright in the bottomless black orbs.

"Answers, damn your beautiful hide," Fargo insisted. "Answers, or you don't get what you want."

"You don't walk out of here alive unless I tell them outside to let you leave," she answered, held her ground, her eyes steady.

Fargo relaxed his grip, let his hand fall to his side. She was as stubborn as she was beautiful. Or as scared. Something had brought her here and had brought him, too. Whatever it was had to be something damn special and damn important to her. Or to somebody.

11

"Are you ready to get on with it now?" she asked almost disdainfully.

Fargo felt the frustrated fury inside him turning into a harsh, angry desire. Maybe there was another way to get the answers he wanted. "I'm ready," he growled. "And you damn well better be." He reached out, pulled the drawstring at the neck of the dress, and the garment fell open, slid from her, to fall at her feet. Fargo felt the touch of awe inside himself as she stood naked before him. It was the nakedness of a statue he had once seen, that of a Greek goddess, clothed in beauty, perfect in every detail. His eyes lingered on the deep, magnificently curved breasts, round and full on the undersides, smoothly curved at the tops. Delicate pink points, surprisingly tiny, were surrounded by small circles of the same faint pink. Her waist narrowed, became rounded hips, a sensuous little belly that curved slightly outward and beneath it, the dense triangle as jet black as the long hair that framed her face. Her legs curved gracefully, her skin milk-white, new-baby smooth.

She stood before him with her face almost expressionless, only the hint of tension in the way her lips pressed upon each other. He took his shirt off and saw her eyes move across his muscled chest, follow downward as he stepped out of trousers, then out of his shorts. He heard the quick intake of her breath, saw the flash in the black eyes, a moment of fascination and fear as her stare stayed on the full beauty of his maleness. She seemed transfixed as, with one hand, he pushed against her and she fell back onto the bed. She came out of it instantly to wriggle away, her breath suddenly harsh.

"Change your mind?" Fargo questioned her wide-eyed stare, and he saw her swallow, shake her head. "Good, because it's too late for that," he said, sinking onto the bed. He drew a deep breath at her beauty. It still didn't make any damn sense, none of it, but whatever the reasons behind it, he was going to enjoy himself. Getting screwed was much better than getting shot. He brought his mouth down onto one beautifully full breast, pulled gently, and heard her long, quivering breath. She started to grow tense, her hands tightened against him, and he felt her force herself to relax. His tongue circled the delicately pink, tiny tip and again he felt her stiffen, force herself to relax. He continued the slow, rotating motion of his tongue and the tiny pink tip began to rise, become a little mound inside his mouth. He closed his teeth on it gently. "Aaaaaah . . ." she murmured, fear and pleasure together in the sound.

His hand moved around the deep breasts, caressing, and then down along her abdomen, down to the dense jet patch. He felt her legs draw together and she seemed to hold herself in until, slowly, she let her legs straighten. She moaned and half-cried out a small sound as his fingers pushed through the dense patch, rubbing, drawing closer to the dark warmth of her, and once again she began to draw her legs up protectively. He pushed his hand between them roughly, fingers entering the warm, dark portal, pushing through. "Aaaah . . . oh . . . iiieee . . . oh," she gasped out, and he heard the pain in her voice. "Quick, oh, quick," she half-screamed, and in her voice there was more desperation than passion.

"No," Fargo said, pulling back. "You're going to enjoy this."

"No, just go on, go on, oh, just go on," she breathed, and he saw the black eyes were almost closed.

He pressed his mouth over the fine-etched lips, pushed his tongue into her mouth until finally she

13

offered a tentative answer. "Quick, oh, please, quick," she murmured.

"Why, I'm not going anyplace," he said.

Her hands came up, grabbed his hair, pulled. "Now, now," she demanded, and once again he heard the angry desperation in her voice. He felt his own fury spiral and he rolled atop her, let his anxious organ find the waiting entranceway. He pushed forward, heard her cry, and felt her flinch, sudden pain, even as he felt the tightness of her around him. "Owoooo . . . oooh, oh . . ." she gasped, and he halted, drew back at once, and her body relaxed, though her hands were little fists against his chest. Her black eyes opened to focus on him as he stared down at her.

"Damn, you're a virgin." Fargo frowned, the surprise real in his voice. She made no reply, looked away, and he continued to stare at her. "I'll be dammed," he muttered.

"What if I am?" she bit out angrily. "I shouldn't think that'd bother you any."

"It doesn't," he said mildly. "It just makes me wonder what the hell you're all about."

"You're not here to wonder. Just get on with it," she said, and her voice rose, a note of demand and desperation moving into it.

"My way," he said, and bent down to take one lovely, full breast in his mouth.

She gasped out at his lips upon her. "Oh, God . . . no, no," she said, and he felt her pull away. "Just do it, just do it," she insisted harshly.

"When and how," he murmured. She shook her head in protest, but he heard her soft cry as his mouth pulled gently at the soft, alabaster-white mound. He gave a tiny half-cry as his hand moved slowly along her lovely body, finding its way to the thick patch to rest there, inch its way to the

14

dark warmth of her. He stroked, caressed, using only slow gentleness. The rigidness came over her again and then began to fade, and she moaned, reluctant protest in the sound. Her breath began to find a rhythm that matched his every slow caress, short little intakes of air with every slow stroke of his hand along the edge of her wet warmth. Words were only sounds now, until unexpectedly he felt her grow rigid, try to fight back.

"No, no, quick, just do it . . . do it . . . oh, no . . ." she cried out, pushed against him, opened her hands, tried to pull him toward her, and he saw the long lovely legs move upward, fall outward, but he only stayed half atop her, stroking, caressing. "Oh, oh . . . oh, God," she breathed, and all her protests and demands became tiny sounds of pleasure. Her body lifted, her legs closing in to grasp his ribs, and her body had taken command, refusing to respond to anything but its own will. And with the sweet urging that was in his hand, his flesh against her, he moved easily, gracefully, slid slowly into her, and felt her stiffen, cry out again, but this time the pain in the cry was mostly an echo. Carefully, gently, he slid forward, back, forward, with a slowness that was excruciating in its pleasure. "Oh, oh, oh . . . ooooh . . . my God, oh, God . . . oh . . ." The words and the sounds flowed into each other as he flowed into her and now her legs were held wide, the portal welcoming, the way smoothed. He felt her hips lift, her body tremble, and he kept to his slow, steady pace, and now she was crying out, trembling sounds, and her fingers closed and unclosed against his back.

He heard the character of her cries suddenly change, a high-pitched, almost fearful sound coming into her voice. She raised her beautiful torso, flung herself against him, up and down in quick succession, and her cries were now overwhelmed by the pure ecstasy of the senses until she screamed, a cry of protest mixed with pleasure, as though she suddenly remembered that she wasn't to enjoy the experience. But enjoyment was past denial now. He had seen to that and she shuddered hard against him, moved almost frantically as the ecstasy of the moment shot through her, overwhelming, filling, obliterating all else.

He stayed inside her as she finally sank back onto the bed and her hands tried to push him away, but they made only feeble motions even as her pelvis writhed to hold him and her legs stayed tight against him. He looked down at the lush, milk-white skin, the magnificent beauty of her, and saw the liquid black eyes open. "Please," she almost whimpered, and he felt her thighs grow limp, fall away from him. He drew from her quickly, roughly, and she cried out as her body reacted to the sudden denial and her legs drew upward in automatic protest. He rose to his knees in front of her, still pulsating, and her eyes stared at him, lingered, her tongue flicking across lips suddenly gone dry.

"The second time's always better," he said, started to move toward her.

"*No!*" The word tore from her and she rolled away, scrambled across the bed to find the dress, fling it over herself. She halted at the far corner of the bed and he waited as she drew in deep, trembling sighs, swallowed hard, glared accusingly at him as her fingers fumbled to tie the drawstring at the neck of the dress.

"Now what was that about not enjoying yourself?" he asked mildly.

"I hated it," she flung back.

"Liar," he returned calmly, and she glowered at him. She swung from the bed, swayed for a moment, then caught herself, straightened, and stepped to the splintered old dresser. She pulled a top drawer open, and when she turned back to him, she was holding a big, long-barreled Anson Chase Colt leveled at his gut. "What's that for?" Fargo frowned.

"Just in case you get the idea to do it again," she said.

"You think of everything, don't you?" he commented.

"Everything," she said, and he peered hard at her. "You've done your part. You'll be free to go now," she told him.

He'd try one more time, he decided. "Why?" he asked. "What the hell does it all mean?"

"It means it's over and you can go," she said, and he caught the hint of bitter weariness in her voice. She stepped to the door but, he noted, kept the old revolver leveled at him. She opened the door just wide enough to call out. "I'm finished with him," she said. "You can let him go now."

She left the door ajar and stepped back as Fargo pulled on clothes and began to walk toward the door. He paused when he reached it, peered hard at her again. Her face was expressionless, a beautiful mask. But he'd not be forgetting Lisa, not even if he had met her under ordinary circumstances. "Till next time, Lisa," he said quietly.

"There won't be a next time," she said. The black orbs held on him and he was certain he detected dark churnings inside their deepness. Her face remained impassive, but she lifted her chin, a touch of pride being pulled back around her. Pride and something else: a hint of dark bitterness. Unreal, all of it, he muttered to himself, wild and weird and beyond believing. But it had been no dream. The warmth of her around him still stayed, the groin furnishing its own proof. He stepped outside, squinted in the sunlight's glare. The four men came toward him, surrounding him, guns in hand.

"The lady said I was free to go," Fargo reminded the short, broad-faced man in front of him.

"That's right, mister," the man agreed. Fargo felt the movement behind him, started to spin, but the gun crashed hard onto his skull and he felt himself drop to one knee, his head made of pain. He knew he pitched forward onto the ground, facedown, and he thought he heard a click of a trigger hammer being pulled back and then consciousness fled, the world becoming a total black vacuum.

3

He was alive. The reassurance came to him out of a distant dimness, more than a feeling yet not a conscious thought. Pain, sharp pinpoints of it pressing into his face, and only the living can feel pain. Slowly he forced his eyes open, waited, let the grayness lighten. The pain against his face persisted and he raised his head. Sharp bits of stone dropped away from his face and the sharp pain ended. Only the throbbing in his head remained. He waited and the pain grew less. Or maybe he was only getting used to it. He grimaced. He pulled his head up straighter and the world tilted, seemed to fall away. He rolled heavily onto his back, rested, let the waves of pain diminish and the world right itself. Finally he sat up, saw the house less than a yard away. There was no need to check inside. The emptiness of it was proclaimed by the open door swinging slowly in a soft wind. His hand touched something at his side and he looked down to see his gun belt, the big Colt .45 in the holster, neatly coiled on the ground alongside him.

He pulled the gun out, checked the chamber. It was fully loaded. He pushed himself to his feet, saw the pinto tethered to a tree nearby. He grunted, grim skepticism in the sound. They'd gone, the girl and the four hired bushwhackers, all vanished, and left him horse and gun. It didn't fit, nothing about it fitted. He let his eyes scan the woodlands. Only a flight of slate-gray catbirds stirred the silence. Fargo's brow wore a deep furrow as he moved on long-legged strides to the striking Ovaro, the horse's jet-black hindquarters and equally black forequarters gleaming in the sunlight.

More than anger dug at the Trailsman. The wild, bizarre incident was shadowed. It hadn't simply been the strange design of a strange, twisted girl. Beautiful Lisa hadn't chosen this way to lose her virginity as a kind of weird whim. He had been hand-picked and there had to be a reason, more than the one she'd so glibly tossed him. He felt danger pulling at him, his wild creature's intuitive senses stirring inside him. They'd gone, but it wasn't over, all of it still made of unanswered questions. Something told him he'd better find out the answers before they found him. He'd been made a part of something and he hadn't the damnedest idea what or why. But he intended to find out before he had any more surprises.

There was only one place to start, by retracing steps back to Wheeltown and a thin blond with a tinkly little-girl voice. He swung his long, hard-muscled frame onto the pinto and started to ride back along the way they'd brought him. He had noted turns, twists, the shapes of trees and rocks, a crook in the path, a cluster of partridge berries, all the things that marked a trail. It had been automatic with him and now he made his way back easily, let his eyes sweep the land. Montana, land of the mountains, first called that by the exploring Spaniards. But virgin land for the most part; this was a place where sudden beauty and sudden death rode side by side. The portion west of the Rockies was included in the

Washington territory, the part east of the mountains counted as part of the Oregon territory. But it really belonged to neither, a land of its own, a place where untamed was not a word but a way of life. Men made their own laws here to let them do whatever they pleased, those lucky enough to survive. Mountain, high plains and fertile forests, dry rock and lush valleys, and all of it deep and rich.

Fargo's eyes peered into the gray-purple distance, picked out the nearest of the individual mountains that were part of the vast and towering Rocky Mountain range, which ran from north to south on a bent axis. He could see Crazy Mountain and, to the west, the Beaverhead Mountains. North, he could make out the parallel peaks of the Little Belt and Big Belt ranges and, beyond, only a faint outline, the towering top of Red Mountain just past Wolf Creek. The red man claimed this Montana land. It was a haven for many tribes: the Flatheads and the Mandans, the Crow, Shoshoni, Assiniboin, northern Cheyenne, and the Gros Ventre, who drifted down from across the Canadian border. But it was the fierce plains Sioux that made the land their own, quick to battle other red men for control, eager to savage the intruding white man.

It was a land best left to those who had their own desperate reasons to take on the wild and the savage. It wasn't a land to chase down a beautiful girl and a puzzle, yet that's what he had to do. Or keep wondering when the unanswered questions would catch up to him and he didn't favor that. He let a harsh laugh escape his lips. Some men came here questing for gold and silver, others for the fortune to be found in fur trapping, and still others hunted a new start in life, but he'd wager that he was the only one seeking a Montana maiden without really knowing why. He spurred the pinto on down a narrow pathway, his lean handsomeness drawn tight with renewed determination. He didn't take to being used, even as a stud.

At the bottom of the path, as the afternoon began to move toward its end, he came upon the place where they'd first taken him. It stood alone, an abandoned shack, and he looked through it, found nothing of help. He remounted the pinto and headed toward Wheeltown in the soft purple of dusk.

It was dark when he reached Wheeltown and he spied the light on in Harry's tannery as he rode past. He'd get back to Harry later, his first stop looming up in front of him as his eyes fastened on the sign THE WHITE SQUAW SALOON. It seemed even more appropriate now, a name he'd not forget easily. He swung from the horse and stepped through the slatted doorway, swept the room in a quick glance that halted on the woman standing at the corner of the plain hardwood bar. Tall, she had a corseted, held-together figure that had perhaps once been generous but now was only blowsy. Her eyes peered at him out of a face no amount of powder and rouge could soften, tight blond curls fixed atop her head as though they'd been lacquered in place. He nodded to the madam as he approached her.

"Remember me?" he asked casually. "I was here last night."

The woman's eyes revealed nothing. "Can't say that I do. But then, I've always had a bad memory for faces," she answered.

Fargo smiled at the bald lie. A madam with a bad memory for faces was like a gopher that didn't know its hole. "I'm looking for Edna," Fargo said pleasantly. "I liked Edna."

The hard face remained expressionless. "Too bad, cowboy. Edna's gone," the woman said. Fargo let his eyebrows lift. "She didn't work out," the madam said. "Can't keep a girl who doesn't make it with the customers."

"Guess not," Fargo said. "Where'd she go?"

"She didn't say and I didn't ask. I'm sure I've got another girl you'd like," the madam said.

Fargo let her have another smile. "I liked Edna," he said, turned, and sauntered out of the saloon. The woman's hard eyes followed him, he knew. The madam of the White Squaw Saloon was lying through her teeth. Had she been paid off, he wondered. Or was she just trying to protect herself and keep possible trouble away? But she was lying. It was all too neat. Edna and her tinkly little-girl voice had cut out too conveniently. But the madam would get a return visit, after the saloon closed. Meanwhile, he headed for Harry McAteer's shop, pulling the pinto along behind him.

Harry was stretching a hide on a wooden rack, he saw as he paused at the window. Harry looked older than he had yesterday, tired and thin. But then Harry had a good fifteen years on him, Fargo reminded himself. When he entered the shop he saw the man turn, a surprised frown flooding his face. "Damn, Fargo, where in hell have you been?" Harry McAteer asked.

"Why?" Fargo questioned.

"I figured you'd show up for coffee this morning. Didn't seem like you to ride out without saying good-bye," the man muttered.

"I was tied up," Fargo said blandly.

He received a pained glance. "You never were one for telling much," the man commented, turned to tighten the rack.

Fargo leaned against the wall. "You get to the saloon often?" he asked.

"Often enough, I guess," Harry answered.

23

"That saloon girl last night, Edna, you know anything about her?" he asked.

"Nope. Never saw her before last night," Harry said.

Fargo's lips pursed, the answer not unexpected. It fitted. Edna had made a one-night appearance with orders to do one thing. "I'll be riding out, Harry," Fargo said. "You stay well, old friend."

The man turned, a moment of ruefulness in his face. "You too, Fargo. It was good remembering, thinking back again," he said.

"Till next time," Fargo returned.

"Don't wait too long. I'm getting older," Harry said, regretfulness in the quick laugh as Fargo slipped out the door. The big black-haired man paused outside for a moment. Nothing good would come from involving Harry McAteer. There'd be time enough for that when he had more answers. He swung onto the Ovaro and rode from town, continued for a half-mile or so, and pulled up under a wide-leafed cottonwood. He dismounted, stretched out on the ground, and watched the moon pull the hours along with it as it slowly moved across the sky. The round, pale sphere was sliding down toward the horizon when he rose and rode slowly back into the town, now a silent, darkened place. Nearing the dark structure that was the saloon, he reined up as he saw the figure standing outside the doorway, a rifle in the crook of his arm. A hard smile passed Fargo's lips for an instant. A guard posted, an affirmation of its own, hardly the thing for cruddy little saloons when they closed. The madam had read the disbelief in his eyes and decided to take no chances.

Fargo turned the pinto into a narrow space between a warehouse and a barber shop, dismounted, left the horse, and moved down along the rear of the few buildings. He emerged at the other corner of the saloon, began to weave and stumble his way down the street. He half-fell, knocked into the cornerpost of the overhang, clung there for a moment, pulled himself upright, and started off again on a drunk's wobbly-legged walk. Head down, he neared the guard in front of the saloon, let himself stagger sideways to slam into the hitching post, bounce off, and go down on one knee almost directly in front of the guard. He seemed to try to pull himself up, but his legs refused to respond and he sprawled forward.

"*Git!*" Fargo heard the man rasp, saw the boot lift, start to hurtle at his side. Fargo held his sprawled position a split second longer and suddenly the uncoordinated, drunken figure twisted away from the vicious kick with precise timing. Powerful arms shot out, yanked the man's leg, pulled, and twisted. The guard's oath was cut off abruptly as the back of his head hit the edge of the wooden step outside the doorway. He tried to roll, shook his head, started to pull himself up when Fargo's blow smashed the butt of the Colt alongside his temple. The man dropped facedown as Fargo caught the rifle, stepped back, and emptied the two cartridges from the chamber. He stepped over the prostrate form lying across the doorway, put the rifle down, and carefully pushed the slatted door inward. A tiny night light from a small lamp in one corner gave the main room a flickering glow as Fargo's eyes swept across the empty tables. It was unlikely there was more than one guard posted, yet he moved carefully. Long ago, he had learned to expect the unexpected.

Satisfied that the room held no surprises, he crossed it to the narrow stairway at the back, mounted the single flight of steps on feet soft and silent as a mountain lion's paws. He paused at the top, squinted down the corridor at the six closed doors, closed his hand around the knob of the first one. He turned the knob slowly and the latch, when it opened, was hardly audible. Peering through the opened door, he closed it as soon as he saw the smallness of the room. The next room was equally small and he moved on to the last room at the far end of the corridor, opened the door an inch, and knew immediately he had the room he sought. It was twice the size of the others, a rolltop desk against one wall, a queen-sized brass bed in the far corner. He slipped inside, silently closed the door after him, and was beside the big bed in three long, noiseless strides.

The woman slept in a nightgown that tried valiantly to contain the heavy, sagging breasts. She snored rhythmically, a heavy, adenoidal sound. Fargo unholstered the Colt, held it in front of her face as he pressed one hand over her mouth. Her eyes came open at once, surprise and sudden fear leaping into their hardness as the first thing she saw was the big barrel of the six-gun in her face. "Screaming can be bad for your health," Fargo said softly. He took his hand from her mouth and the madam pushed herself up to a sitting position, her eyes still on the gun in her face. "Now you're going to tell me about Edna," Fargo said.

Her eyes moved from the gun. "I told you," she muttered. Fargo's hand shot out, seized hold of the nightgown, yanked the woman forward with such force that her head bobbed back and forth.

"The truth, goddamnit," he demanded. "And you can forget about your stupid sentry boy." He twisted the top of the nightgown, saw it cut into the woman's neck.

"You're choking me," she sputtered.

"Not yet, but I'm thinking about it," Fargo growled.

Fargo saw her trying to read his eyes and he

26

twisted the top of the nightgown harder. She swallowed, felt breath growing difficult. Her lips moved, but only a rasping sound came from them and Fargo loosened his grip. The woman gasped in air gratefully.

"She wanted to be one of my girls for one night, she told me," the madam said.

"And you just hired her," Fargo sneered.

The hard eyes glowered at him. "She paid me good money for it," the madam said.

"What else?" he asked.

"Nothing else," the woman said.

Fargo's hand tightened the nightgown again, saw it cut into the woman's neck. "You didn't just agree, not your kind. You asked questions. What'd she tell you, dammit?" he rasped, saw the cords of the woman's neck begin to bulge. He twisted his hand another half-inch and the woman moved her lips as only a wheeze escaped her. He relaxed his grip enough for her to get air again.

"She said she had something to do," the woman said. "A man she was waiting for."

"What else?" Fargo pressed.

"Nothing else. She said there wouldn't be any trouble."

"She was almost right," Fargo said, his eyes narrowing at the woman. She licked her lips nervously. "Where'd she go?" he asked.

"I don't know. She just lit out," the woman said.

"Where'd she come from?" he questioned.

"Don't know," the madam said, but he caught the split-second hesitation in her voice. His hand tightened on the nightgown at once, harder this time, and the woman's eyes began to bulge. She tried to swallow, feebly waved a hand, and he relaxed his grip again.

27

"Indian Creek, that's what she told me," the woman gasped out. "That's all I know, honest."

"You wouldn't know how to spell honest," Fargo said as his thoughts raced. Indian Creek was a nothing village to the south. He'd passed through it with the wagonload of settlers. They'd stopped for a bag of flour there. He frowned, muttered a silent oath. It didn't make any more sense than the rest of what had happened. He took his hand from the nightgown and the madam's face flooded with relief.

"I don't know anything more about her," she said, rubbing her neck with one hand.

Fargo straightened, his eyes ice-cold on the woman. "I'll be back if you're lying," he warned, and she glared back, but there was fear in her eyes and he was reasonably sure she had told him the truth. He moved from the room as quickly and silently as he had come, hurried down the dark stairway. Outside, the guard still lay unconscious and Fargo walked to where he had left the pinto. Minutes later he was riding out of Wheeltown as the morning began to sweep the night away.

He rode south, found a spot in a stand of oaks, and caught a few hours of sleep in the coolness of their shade and was heading south again by the time the noon sun rose directly overhead. He spotted a line of riders in the distance, horsemen moving in single file across a ridge, and he made a wide, swinging detour. The land rose, thick forests of gambel oak and red ash, lush and rich. He reached Indian Creek as the day began to slide away. The small creek that gave the village its name wandered idly along the back edge of a handful of frame buildings, the first a blacksmith shop. Fargo halted, saw the leather-aproned man eye the beauty of the Ovaro with instant appreciation.

"Looking for Edna," Fargo said casually. "Know where I might find her?"

"Edna Corrigan?" the man asked.

"How many Ednas do you have in a place this size?" Fargo asked, more sharply than he'd intended.

"Happens we've got two," the smithy said.

"Thin, washed-out blonde," Fargo said. "Sounds like a ten-year-old."

"That'd be Edna Corrigan, all right," the man replied. "Reckon she'd still be at the store at this hour. Nice girl, Edna."

"The best," Fargo said, and walked the pinto forward. The town store, a narrow building, stood in the very center of the town; Fargo dismounted to one side of it, approached the door from along the wall of the building. His eyes took in the interior of the general store in one quick glance as he stepped inside. Two portly women huddled over a bolt of linsey-woolsey and a white-haired man poked through a barrel of tenpenny nails, but there was no thin, washed-out blonde. A back room was partly visible behind a long counter and suddenly he heard the voice from the room, a tinkly little-girl voice, a voice impossible to mistake for any other. As he watched, a woman with thick eyeglasses emerged from the back room, went over to the man beside the barrel of nails. Fargo's eyes were still on the doorway as the girl emerged. He ducked behind a stack of boxes at once, watched her start to come around the counter, no low-necked, tight dance-hall girl's dress now but a very proper dark-red gingham gown. He stepped from behind the boxes as she neared.

"Remember me?" he asked softly, but his eyes were blue quartz.

She stared at him and he saw her eyes widen in

29

shock, slide into near panic. She cast a furtive glance around the store. "Please, not here," she whispered.

"Where?" he growled.

She stared at him for another moment. She was prettier than he'd remembered in a pale way, blond hair a little stringy, prettier and taller, her nose straight, lips a little thin, like the rest of her. The small breasts made tiny mounds under the gingham gown. "I'll get my bag," she said, the tinkly little-girl voice growing stronger. "I know where we can talk. Just give me a moment."

He nodded, and she spun, disappeared into the back room. He tossed a glance at the other woman who was waiting on the man beside the nail barrel. The two portly women still huddled over the bolt of yard goods and his eyes moved to the doorway of the back room. The thin figure didn't come into sight. He waited a moment more and she still didn't emerge, and suddenly the frown dug into his brow. He felt the oath gathering deep inside him and he skirted the end of the counter with one long stride, stepped through the door frame to the back room. "Sir, you can't go in there," he heard the woman call out as he halted, his eyes sweeping the room.

"Tend to your customers," he growled without looking at her. The room was full of extra stock, boxes, barrels, bolts of yard goods, but no thin, tall blonde, and his eyes spied the back door. It was still ajar and the oath that had gathered inside him exploded into sound. *"Goddamn!"* he roared. "Sneaking little bitch." Swerving around stacks of boxes, he yanked the back door open, found himself at the rear of the building, staring out at the dimness of dusk and empty space. A short hitching post protruded from the corner of the building and he was beside it in one long stride.

He knelt, his eyes agate-hard as they examined

the ground. He made a grunting noise as he saw the marks, hoofprints dug into the ground, a horse being turned in a tight circle, sent off at a gallop. He rose, ran back to where he'd left the pinto. The other woman was at the back door, looking confused, when he raced the pinto between the buildings, his eyes following the hoofmarks in the dry soil. They led to the little creek a dozen yards away and he reined to a halt at the edge of it. She was trying to be clever. She'd leaped the creek to avoid leaving wet hoofmarks, but his trailsman's eyes quickly spotted the marks deeper in the soil where the horse's hooves had landed. He sent the pinto on across the little creek and saw that her hoofmarks led straight north into the wooded land. She was riding the horse full out, he saw. He also saw that he hadn't more than a half-hour of dusk left.

Reaching the woodlands, he slowed as he entered the forest, the light inside it almost gone. But he could see the edges of the brush where it had been pushed back, and he picked out the low, thin tree branches snapped off. She was still riding hard, counting on a head start and the night closing too quickly for him to pick up her trail. Proof you could be thin and fatheaded at the same time, he grunted as he sent the pinto in pursuit. He bent low in the saddle, straining his eyes in the half-light to pick up the path of the racing horse. She had passed through a heavy cluster of buckthorn, the heavy holly leaf slow to bend back, marking a clear trail, and he spurred the pinto on faster, saw where she had made a sharp change in course. It was a poorly thought-out move, he commented silently. It hadn't thrown him off at all and the pinto could move through the thick buckthorn with greater ease than the average saddle horse.

The woods began to thin, became a rolling, grassy

plain, and he saw her, only a few hundred yards ahead. He sent the pinto full out and closed the distance quickly. The girl heard him coming, glanced back, her face strained and the washed-out blond hair streaming out straight behind her. He saw her slap her reins against the horse's neck, but it was a futile effort. Her mount was running out of steam and Fargo caught her a dozen yards from the next wooded area, grasped hold of her horse's cheek strap, and pulled the animal to a halt. The girl leaped from the saddle, fell, and before she could fully regain her feet, Fargo had hold of her. She blinked at him and he saw fright in her eyes. They were a pale blue, he noticed for the first time.

"I was paid to do it," she blurted out.

Fargo kept his hold on her arm. "That's getting to be the stock answer here," he said.

She blinked her pale-blue eyes again. "What's that mean?" she asked tentatively.

"The madam said you paid her and now you say somebody paid you. Try again, honey," Fargo growled.

She licked her lips. "It's true," she said.

"Really? Well, now, Edna, honey, suppose you start from the beginning. Who paid you?" Fargo asked.

"A man."

"What man?"

"Never saw him before."

"He have a name?"

"He didn't say."

"But he paid you to put knockout drops in my drink?"

She nodded.

"He say why?"

"No."

Fargo half-smiled, her answers all so very convenient. The tinkly little-girl voice had a way of making everything she said sound believable. Only, he knew better. He let his lips purse. "Now, let's take that again, Edna," he began. "This man with no name just comes out of nowhere, pays you to play a saloon girl and put knockout drops in my drink, and you agree. You're very agreeable, aren't you, Edna?"

She half-glowered from under lowered eyelids. "It was a lot of money," she said.

"And that story's a lot of cowshit," Fargo snapped. "You don't really expect me to buy it, do you?" She continued to glower at him. His hand shot out, yanked her forward roughly. "How about a beautiful girl paid you," he rasped. "I like that better. A beautiful girl named Lisa. Who is she and why me, dammit?"

"I don't know what you're talking about," Edna said, fear making her little-girl voice sound even smaller.

"Hell you don't," Fargo snapped, let her go, and she took a quick step backward and the fear stayed in her eyes behind the glower. "You're too young to have such a bad memory, Edna. You can work on it while we ride," Fargo told her.

"Ride where?" she asked, the alarm quick in her voice.

"North, the way you were heading. Maybe you were doing more than just running away. Maybe you were trying to reach her," Fargo mused aloud.

"No," Edna said quickly, but he caught the alarm rise in her voice.

Fargo's smile was made of ice. "Then we'll just ride till your memory comes back," he said.

He saw her swallow. "I told you all I know," she said.

"I'm just naturally hard to convince," Fargo said. "On your horse." He half-turned, pulled himself up

33

on the pinto as the last of the dusk trickled away and the night surrounded them.

The little voice told big lies, he was certain. He took the reins of her horse, wrapped them around his saddle horn so that she had to ride close beside him. Edna was his one lead. He'd take no chances of losing it. He watched her climb onto the horse, small breasts pressing tiny curves into the gingham dress as she sat very straight in the saddle. Her face was tense but her lips were set in stubbornness. "Maybe you ought to tell me something about yourself," Fargo said as he moved the horses into the forest. "It might help your memory."

"There's nothing to tell," she muttered.

"I'd bet there is," Fargo said blandly. "Like what's a nice girl like you doing playing whore?"

"The money, I told you," she said sharply.

His smile was rejection. "Well, you never did get the chance to finish playing whore. We can take care of that," he said evenly, drew a quick, sharp glance from her. He turned his eyes ahead, his handsome, intense face expressionless, and she fell silent, rode beside him for another fifteen minutes until he halted where two thick-trunked black oaks had let a little circle form between them. "We'll camp here till morning," he announced.

"You let me go," he heard Edna say as he swung from the pinto.

"Your memory getting any better?" he asked.

"I've no nightclothes. I'll freeze," she protested.

"I've an extra blanket," he said. "Off the horse." Edna glared at him as she swung down, but he caught a glimpse of her long legs, which had been so much more revealed in the saloon-girl dress. They were still the best part of her, he grunted inwardly. He made a small fire, just enough to brew some coffee and heat the piece of salted pork in his saddlebag. The mountain night grew cool quickly, as always, and the tiny fire was welcome. He handed her a tin cup of coffee and she took it silently, said nothing more when she accepted the piece of warmed pork.

"If I didn't know better, I'd think you were angry about something, Edna," Fargo commented as he stretched out on the ground. She tossed him a glare, drew her legs up, and sat silently in front of the small fire, finished sipping the coffee after she downed the meat. He rose, took the extra blanket from his saddle roll, and handed it to her. She got to her feet, holding the blanket in front of her, watched him unstrap his gun belt, start to undo his trousers. "You figure to sleep in that dress?" he asked.

She spun around, her face tightly set, and marched into the blackness of the surrounding trees. He was in his shorts atop his own blanket when she returned, the gingham dress in one hand, the blanket wrapped completely around her in Indian fashion. She lay down on the opposite side of the dying fire, stretched out, keeping the blanket fully covering her. Fargo let the fire burn down to a few glowing sticks before he rose and stepped to where she lay wrapped in the blanket. She turned to look up at him and he saw her eyes move across his powerful, beautifully modeled body, lingering for a moment at the bulge under his shorts. She blinked, brought her glance away, frowned as she saw the lariat in his hand. "What's that for?" she asked, alarm coming into her eyes.

"Just to make sure you don't get any ideas. I want to get some sleep without having to stay awake to watch you," he said. "Hold out your wrists."

"No," she said. "I won't be tied up."

35

"Just your wrists. It won't bother your sleeping," he said.

"No," she snapped again, started to pull away, clinging to the blanket.

"Dammit, I'm not going to spend the night arguing with you," Fargo roared, reached out and ripped the blanket down from her, and heard her short gasp of protest. She wore only a half-chemise under the blanket and his eyes took in her naked torso, lithe, thin, a narrow waist. Little-girl breasts to go with her little-girl voice. Toy tits, he found himself thinking, yet strangely attractive, pointy little mounds, firm and milk-white with pink circles and very red little points. Her thinness was more than thinness, a supple, tight, smooth body, and she started to bring her arms up to cover herself, but he caught her wrist, yanked her forward.

He had the lariat around it in moments, then her other wrist and her hands were tied securely in front of her while she was still gathering words of protest. "I won't be able to sleep this way," she said.

"You can sleep fine. You can turn any way you like. You can even pull the blanket up with your fingers," he said, and she took his words, reached down, and pulled the blanket over herself at once. "Just remember that the other end of the rope will be in my hand, so don't get any ideas of running," Fargo told her. "Sleep tight, Edna," he said almost cheerfully. Taking the end of the lariat with him, he settled down under his own blanket, wrapped the end of the lariat around one wrist. He watched Edna turn on her side and wondered where she really fit in the damn puzzle. She'd stayed hard-nosed so far, but he'd noticed that she was not without fear. Maybe a night to think it over would loosen her tongue, he pondered, closed his eyes, and slept in moments, the big Colt close beside him.

He slept soundly, woke only twice as he felt the rope on his wrist pull, but Edna was only turning in her sleep under the blanket. He woke first, just as the new sun was starting to filter down through the forest canopy of leaves. He unrolled the rope from his wrist, took his canteen, and washed. He'd just finished when Edna woke, sat up, pulling the blanket high in front of her. Her eyes found him with an instant glower, and still clad only in shorts, he went to her and untied her wrist ropes. His outlined maleness under the shorts was directly at eye level with her and he saw her stare, wrench her eyes away, and get to her feet with the blanket held around her. He handed her the canteen. "Use the rest of it. I'll refill it along the way someplace," he said, and drew on trousers as she went into the trees with the gingham dress and the blanket still wrapped around her.

He was on the pinto when she emerged, the blanket folded over one arm, and he found himself frowning as she came toward him. She had her own attractiveness, a kind of thin, washed-out look that reminded him of a picture all done in pale pastel colors. He took the blanket from her, put it into his saddle roll as she climbed onto the horse alongside him. "We'll ride some before the sun sets to burning," he said, moved the pinto forward, the reins of the other horse still wrapped around his saddle horn. He followed a trail that led upwards and out onto a cleared ridge. A good part of the morning had passed when he came upon a wild-plum bush and halted to enjoy a sweet, cool breakfast. "Your memory come back any?" he asked mildly.

Edna halted in devouring one of the plums. "No," she said.

He gave her a thin smile. "Then we'll just keep heading north," he said. He quickened the pace a

37

little when they began riding again. They'd ridden past the noon hour when two riders appeared, a little below on the side of a grassy slope. Edna pulled her horse to a halt at once, started to push back under the tree cover nearby, and he saw the fear that had leaped into her eyes. He let the pinto move under the trees with her, watched the two riders disappear down the slope.

"What was all that about?" he asked.

She blinked at him, recovered her composure. "What do you mean?" she returned, her tinkly little-girl voice sounding so terribly innocent.

"You looked at those two cowhands as though you were seeing a Sioux war party," Fargo said.

"They surprised me, that's all," Edna said.

Fargo nodded and kept the words on his tongue to himself. Edna was handing him another cock-and-bull story. She could have cried out, yelled for help before he'd been able to stop her, the two cowhands close enough to hear. But she had stayed silent, silent and scared as hell. Why? he thought, frowning, moved the horses forward again. She wanted to get away from him, yet two passing riders had scared her into silence. It didn't make any sense. But nothing about this damn puzzle made sense. But he was more certain than ever that he'd better find out the answers.

It was a little more than an hour later when he heard the tinkly little-girl voice call his name. "Fargo, you've got to let me go," she began. "I've got a job. I'll be fired if I just disappear."

"Sure you can go," he said, and saw her eyes grow wide. "Soon as your memory comes back," he finished. The wide eyes became hard with anger. "It's your game, Edna, honey. Whenever you're ready," he said, and she looked away, her mouth setting it-

38

self. She said nothing more until he came to a stretch of high plains and turned west on it.

"Why this way?" she blurted out, and surprise didn't hide the alarm in her voice.

"It's more likely she's this way than in the high country," he answered, and saw her eyes narrow and she became glumly silent again. He watched her through the rest of the afternoon, saw the way her eyes caught at every little thing that moved, alarm instant in their pale orbs each time. By the time the day began to slide toward an end he'd seen her face slide from emotion to emotion, from unhappy to angry, fear to stubbornness, and her mood became one of increasing nervousness. A wide river appeared, curving around a line of heavy bur oak, and he halted at the bank. His glance swept the water, which appeared quietly flowing on the surface, but he spotted the ripples that dotted the water, saw a submerged tree branch bending. A fierce current ran just under the surface and he wagered that around the bend the river became rushing white water. He listened, caught the faint sound of a quiet roar, and started to wheel the pinto away from the bank.

"We're not crossing?" Edna asked in surprise.

"Not here. There's a strong undercurrent. The horses would sink down into it and it'd sweep them downriver," Fargo said. "We'll make camp here, find another spot come morning." He swung from the pinto as Edna dismounted, handed her his canteen. "Fill it while I get a fire going," he said.

She walked toward the riverbank with the canteen as he gathered small twigs and a half-dozen larger pieces of wood. He cast a glance at Edna as he began to work on getting a fire started, saw her kneeling at the water's edge, filling the canteen. He concentrated on his task when he heard the faint sound of the water, a quiet half-splash, half-ripple. He looked up and heard the oath fall from his lips. She was swimming hard, striking out for the opposite shore.

"Don't be a damn fool," he shouted as he ran to the bank. But she was a good swimmer, he saw, her thin form cleaving the water with strength and speed. "Damn fool girl," he muttered again, watched as she neared midriver, saw her suddenly slow, her figure half-turn around in the water. She pumped her arms, started to right herself, but she was turned again, spun around completely this time, and he caught the moment of surprise on her face. The undercurrent had seized her and Fargo swore silently as she pumped her arms, tried to fight the undercurrent only to find herself being pulled downriver. She was flailing now, panic and desperation taking over. She'd tire herself out completely in another minute, he knew, and he turned, raced to the pinto, and vaulted into the saddle.

He cast another glance at her, saw her arms slowing as her strength faded. She was moving downriver quickly now, the current pulling her in its inexorable grip. She turned on her back to float and rest a moment, and now she was being swept along the water. She'd be carried around the bend in minutes and Fargo cursed silently at the precious moments he had to spend unwrapping her horse's reins from around his saddle horn. She was just being carried around the bend when he finished, flung the reins aside, and sent the pinto racing along the edge of the riverbank. He glimpsed the pale-blond hair disappearing around the bend and sent the pinto all out into the curve of the bank.

"Shit," he muttered as he rounded the other side of the curve. Just ahead, not more than a dozen yards away, the river became a roaring rapids of foaming white water that cascaded over a bed of heavy boulders. As he raced past Edna, he glimpsed the terror in her face as, helpless now, she saw the turbulent fury of the water as it raced over the rocks. Damn fool girl, Fargo swore as he raced the pinto forward. The raging water would smash her into the rocks with deadly, bone-shattering force. As he reached the bank opposite the first line of rocks, he leaped from the saddle, lariat in hand, plunged into the water near the shore, and felt the force of it grab at his legs at once. He braced himself as a shower of spray hit his face; he swung the lariat in a fast circle. Edna was being pulled with furious speed now, and he saw the thin figure disappear for a moment, bob into view again beside a foam of water. He tossed the lariat with all the strength and skill he possessed, watched it hit the racing water, half around Edna. She reached out, grasped hold of it before the water tore it away, and he took another moment to let her get two hands on the rope. When he started to pull, he felt her body and the force of the water seem to increase tenfold. He pulled the rope in toward him as his eyes measured the angle to the first of the rocks.

He swore silently. The water was swinging her in a half-arc as he pulled, swinging her forward toward a huge rock where the foam leaped high in angry whiteness. Fargo pulled frantically, felt his shoulder muscles bunching up with the strain, growing close to cramping on him. It'd be close, he saw, too close. Edna saw it, too, and her face held only stark terror now. Fargo took a step toward the riverbank as he pulled at the rope, felt the fury of the water as it refused to be cheated of a victim. He managed another step as he continued to reel in the lariat. The inches helped, shortened the angle of the arc, and again he fought the force of the rushing water in a deadly tug-of-war, furiously gathering the rope in as Edna swung toward the rock. His lips drew back as he saw her blond hair bouncing on the water, about to smash into the rock and the foaming whitewater that sprayed from it. He yanked again, felt himself falling backward, and he hit the water, went under for a moment, but not before he caught the glimpse of Edna's head go past the rock with not more than a fraction of an inch to spare.

He pulled himself to one knee, yanked again at the rope, felt his hands slip with wetness, but kept on, every muscle in his back and shoulders protesting. He took another step, got one foot into the soft soil of the riverbank, climbed upward as he continued to reel in the lariat. He was on the bank, both feet pressing deep into the soft soil as he saw the thin form reach the shoreline, claw her way forward on hands and knees. She fell forward onto the dry bank, and he toppled over backward, joined her in drawing in deep gasping breaths. He lay there, let his muscles slack in the aftermath of pain as his breath came back to normal.

When he pulled himself to a sitting position, he saw Edna's pale-blue eyes on him as she raised her head. "I thought I'd be light enough to stay above the undercurrent," the tinkly little-girl voice said.

"You make a lot of mistakes, don't you?" he answered between deep breaths. Her wet clothes clung to her and he saw her shiver. He got to his feet, reached a hand out, and pulled her up. "Get on the pinto," he growled as he coiled the lariat, swung into the saddle behind her, and felt himself shiver as the dusk winds began to swirl. He sent the pinto back around the curve to where he'd started to make camp.

"I'd be smashed to bits if it weren't for you," Edna murmured, her voice even smaller than usual.

"Don't let it go to your head," he said roughly. "We've things to talk about, remember?"

She turned her head, looked back at him, and the pale-blue eyes were wide. "You still did it, saved my life," she said.

"Just one of those things," he said, reined up at the campsite, and swung from the pinto. He helped her down and she squished water over him; he felt her shiver. "Get out of those wet clothes. Everything," he said. "They're making you even colder."

She walked to the edge of the oaks and he shed his own shirt and trousers as he worked to get the fire started again. He took off the shorts as the fire caught, sent a wonderfully welcome rush of warmth over him. He rose, got the blankets from his saddle roll, and put them on the ground, peered at the line of trees and saw her there, arms covering herself, half-hidden behind the leaves.

"Get the hell over here before you freeze to death. You can't dry out over there," he said.

"Give me a blanket," she asked.

"Hell, you'll just get it all wet now and then it'll be no use to you. After you dry off," he told her, saw her hesitate, and he rose, took a step toward her. "Dammit, get over here," he said. Modesty gave way to her shivering coldness and she came forward, fell to her knees before the fire, reached her arms out to let the warmth flow over her. Her little-girl breasts seemed entirely appropriate as she knelt in nakedness, her body supple, a slender waist, almost straight hips, and just the tiniest curvature of a belly, long, lovely legs, and surprisingly, a very large, very black triangle, the thick luxuriousness of it not at all in keeping with the rest of her. But once again, she commanded her own attractiveness. Kneeling before the fire, she seemed some sort of woodland sprite, a fawnlike quality to her.

43

She lifted her eyes to meet his gaze, straightened her back, and let the little breasts rise proudly, a sudden, very sensuous femaleness sweeping over her, and he felt the stirring in his loins. Her glance fell to where the inner stirrings translated themselves into a rising, pulsating vibrancy, and he saw her lips part, her tongue flick over the edge of her upper lip. He felt the surge of excitement spiral inside him. Unexpected beauty brings its own excitement, the wanting of discovery, and he saw her lean toward him, her arms lifting, sliding around his neck. She came against him, dry and warm now, the tiny points pushing into his chest, excitingly firm. He leaned back onto the blanket and she came with him, her mouth pressing hard against his and her tongue darting forward instantly. Her thin body rubbed against him, the long, supple legs curling half around him as he rolled her on her back, let his own tongue meet hers, circling, a soft contest of sensuousness. His thumb brushed across one of the tiny, very red nipples and he felt her quiver at once, her entire body responding.

"Aaaaah . . . ah, ah, yes," she murmured, the little-girl voice suddenly octaves lower, a soft, husky murmur. He lowered his mouth, took the little breast into it, and felt the tiny tip almost spring upright instantly. He all but swallowed the breast and felt Edna Corrigan's body shaking as her hands clutched at him, opening and closing against his back. He moved half over her, kept hold of the little breast, drawing gently on it as she made little murmuring noises; he ran both hands down along her body, past the narrow waist, across both hips, moved inward, and pressed his fingers into the thick black nap. Again she cried out, this time her voice rising, a half-scream of anticipation. His one hand moved to cup around her buttocks, his hand all but encircling one softly firm mound as he rubbed through the luxurious triangle with his other hand. Her long legs moved outward and her pelvis rose, thrust upward as she dug both heels into the ground, the invitation demanding, and a cry of anxiety came from her lips.

"Please, please, oh, yes . . . oh, please," she said, lifting higher for him. He brought his gift to the very tip of her warm darkness and held there, moving slowly, a faint touch of wetness against wetness, burning flesh against quivering lips.

"Aaaaah, oh, God," she almost screamed, flung herself upward as her hands pulled at him. "Yes, yes . . . oh, please," she cried out, and he held a moment longer, heard her half-sobbed scream, and plunged forward, deep into the enveloping warmth of her. Edna Corrigan's supple body seemed to become a snake as she writhed, twisted, long legs clasping and unclasping, then clasping again around him. Her hair fell from side to side and low, husky sounds came from her, almost guttural. She pushed up and down with his every movement until, with unexpected quickness, her hands smashed against his ribs and she went high into the air with him and the scream tore from her throat, no little-girl voice now, but a full-throated cry of despair and ecstasy made one. He let himself explode with her and her tiny breasts quivered with the tremors that ran through her. "My God, oh, my God," she breathed. "Yes, oh, yes, aaaaa-a-a-iiieeee . . . oh, yes." She held him to her as the quivering lessened, finally stopped, and she fell back onto the blanket, drawing in deep gasps of air. Her legs stayed tight around his hips, clasping him inside her, and he stayed with her, let his mouth take in first one little breast, then the other. Finally he felt her legs fall aside and he lay down half over her, watched her open her pale-

45

blue eyes to stare up at him as though she were returning to the world from a distant place.

He rolled onto his back, pulled her over atop him,
and drew the blanket up around their nakedness.
The twin little points, surprisingly hard, pushed into
his chest. "You explode suddenly, don't you?" Fargo
commented.

"Not usually," she murmured, sounding like a
little girl again.

"It was more than saying thanks," he remarked.

"I know. It was wanting, the burning kind. It just
came over me. Maybe it was seeing you this way.
Maybe it's just been too long. Whatever it was, it
was worth it," she said. Her thin frame seemed
hardly a weight atop him and he rested one hand
across the small of her back. Instantly she uttered a
little sigh and pressed the thick black triangle into
him. Her pale-blue eyes peered deeply. "I'm sorry
for what I did back in Wheeltown," she said. "Honestly I am."

"Sorry enough to start telling the truth?" he
asked.

She pushed herself to a sitting position and the
blanket fell to her waist and suddenly she was a
thing of fawnlike loveliness again. He watched her
small face grow grave, almost pouting. "Her name's
Lisa Toomis," she said quietly.

Fargo peered at her, saw the honesty in her eyes.
"Go on," he said.

"She came to me at the store, told me what she
wanted, and offered good money, too good to just
turn down," Edna said, paused, groped for words. "I
didn't know you'd be . . . well, like you are. I
thought you'd be some trail bum."

"You know her before she came to you?" Fargo
questioned.

"No, not really, but I'd seen her in town, always

with those two idiot Toomis boys," Edna said. Her lips tightened for a moment. "She is beautiful, the most beautiful girl I've ever seen."

"You know where she lives?" he asked.

"The other side of the river. You go straight till you reach a doubled-over rock, turn north there," Edna said.

"What the hell does it all mean? Why me?" Fargo frowned.

Edna's eyes widened a fraction. "She never said. I just supposed you'd done her wrong somewhere, sometime."

"I'd remember if I had," Fargo said with a touch of ruefulness.

The girl's small face took on a furrow. "Then what was it all about?" she asked.

"A lot less than it seemed, a lot more than it was," he answered, and knew his reply was too cryptic for her to gather in.

Edna's face stayed grave. "I know one thing more," she said. "I heard you're a dead man. Anyone with you, too." She came forward, pressed the small breasts against his chest. "Why don't you forget about her? Run, get away from here," she said.

"Don't like running and don't like unanswered questions," he told her as he saw the concern real and open in the pale-blue eyes. He brushed a strand of washed-out blond hair from her face. "Thanks." He smiled. "Can you find your way back to Indian Creek come morning?"

She nodded, pressed herself tighter against him, and he felt her hand moving slowly up along the inside of his thigh. "Come morning," she whispered, her hand closing around him, soft and firm at once, sweet grip that evoked his instant response, and he felt the swelling begin inside the cup of her hand. "Oh, God, come morning," she breathed, began to

47

stroke gently, moving her hands up and down along the growing, swelling beauty of him, and she brought one leg over, pressed the black triangle against him, rubbed it back and forth over his organ as little murmurings came from her and he felt her legs being drawn upward. Her pelvis turned, pushed, sought the object made for its dark and waiting portal. It was a seeking that quickly became frantic and he moved, helped her find the fulfillment she sought. She sank over him at once as a groan of eternal satisfaction came from deep inside her. Small, intense, gyrating movements began at once as her body quivered, and it seemed she sought to push him into the deepest corners of her, to fill herself hungrily with his vibrant flesh.

The sounds of her murmured and gasped pleasure encompassed the night once again as he gave all she wanted and more, and finally she lay beside him, one long leg atop his torso, her thin body still in the sleep of the exhausted.

4

He woke first with the morning, began to pull on clothes, and was dressed when she came awake and sat up. She stretched and suddenly looked very little-girl again. When she finished dressing, her small face was set tightly; the pale-blue eyes held a kind of rueful acceptance and she peered at him, not smiling, a long, probing look.

"What if you don't find those answers?" she asked.

"I'll find them," he said.

"If you don't, I'll be in Indian Creek," she said in her tinkly little voice.

"I'll remember that," he told her, and she gave a half-smile that said she didn't really believe him. She climbed onto her horse, turned slowly, and moved away, not looking back. He watched her go until she was out of sight. She had been a creature of surprises, of very womanly passion behind the wan, washed-out appearance and that little-girl voice. And she could turn into a surprisingly attractive wood nymph, but she'd been only a pawn in a puzzle that needed answers more than ever now. He mounted the pinto and began to ride north till he found a spot to cross the river, his thoughts already turned to finding a beautiful enigma.

His eyes swept the terrain for the mark Edna had

called the doubled-over rock, and he'd ridden a few miles when he saw the two riders cutting across a gentle slope in the land just in front of him. He saw the two men turn in their saddles, focus on him as he rode toward them. Fargo waved an arm in greeting. "Ho, there," he called out. "I'm looking for doubled-over rock."

"Goddamn, it's him," he heard one of the riders half-shout, felt the frown dig into his forehead as both men yanked six-guns. Fargo dropped low to one side as the first shots whistled over his head. He wheeled the pinto, staying low in the saddle, and sent the horse racing for a clump of Rocky Mountain maple a dozen yards away. He rode half-hanging from the saddle, hidden by the pinto from the second fusillade of shots that exploded. He dived from the saddle as the pinto charged into the trees, hit the ground rolling, to come up in the brush with the big Colt .45 in his hand.

The two horsemen raced off in opposite directions, heading into the maples, one to his left, the other to his right. They had ideas of sandwiching him between them, he saw; he pushed back deeper into the underbrush and heard the two men jump down from their horses. He settled down, became fixed, motionless, letting his acute hearing reach out. The two men were starting to move toward him' from both sides. He remained motionless, listening.

They were moving slowly, carefully, pausing to halt and peer around every few steps, then move forward again. Fargo followed their every movement with his ears, the way a bobcat traces a chipmunk without seeing him. He lay hardly breathing, every fiber of his body tuned to listening, a man of wild-creature instincts, his every sense sharpened, his entire body tingling with a waiting that was really just another form of action.

The sounds began to separate. The man on his left was moving a little faster than the other, growing too hasty. Fargo's lips formed a smile of ice. The man came in a straight line now, halting to listen, peer ahead. Fargo remained absolutely motionless, lying flat, only his head raised just enough to see the man's form appear moving through the trees toward him. Fargo waited, lifted the big Colt, a slow, silent movement. His ears caught the sound of the second man nearing from the other side, suddenly hurrying, too. He drew a bead on the nearest figure in his sight. He'd have chance for only one shot to avoid being caught in a cross fire. Even then, his first shot would mark his position and he readied himself for that. He dug his feet into the ground, curling his toes against the soil, tightening powerful leg muscles.

The nearest man in his sight appeared more clearly, moving through a lacy network of small branches. Fargo's finger tightened on the trigger as he waited a moment longer, let the man's bulk grow closer. Drawing his lips back, he pulled the trigger and the silence exploded with the heavy sound of the big Colt. He had time only to glimpse the figure start to catapult backward, hands clawing out in the air, a choking roar coming from the man's throat, and then he was throwing himself to one side as the volley of shots erupted, slammed into the ground where he'd lain in wait. He kept rolling as the second attacker continued to shoot, trying to follow the sound of his movements.

Fargo heard the shots halt for a moment as the man reloaded. He came up against a tree trunk, flung himself around it as the second attacker charged forward again. The man fired wildly, laying down a scattered barrage ahead of himself. Fargo took careful aim, his finger poised on the trigger.

"Drop the gun," he called out.

The man halted, paused, froze in motion for a moment. Fargo watched him start to lower his gun hand. He had just relaxed the pressure on the Colt's trigger when the man dropped flat, facedown, his gun blasting off a volley of shots. They slammed into the tree trunk, tearing away bits of bark a fraction from his head. The man had regained his feet, charged forward as he lay down a cover of fire that sprayed the tree. Fargo dropped low, blasted off two shots as the man whirled toward him. He saw the figure stumble forward, lurch through the brush as if suddenly drunk, smash into a tree, and sink to the ground. Fargo waited till he saw the man topple away from the tree, his gun falling from lifeless fingers.

"Damn!" Fargo muttered as he holstered the Colt. He'd wanted answers and these two wouldn't answer anyone anymore. He examined both bodies, went through pockets. One had a receipt for a tarpaulin that carried his name on it. "Abner Ammon," Fargo read aloud, frowned. The name meant nothing to him. But both men had known him at once, started shooting instantly. Why? He frowned as he returned to the pinto. Why had two men he'd never seen before start blazing away at him? A case of mistaken identity? He turned the thought in his mind. He couldn't dismiss it, but his gut feelings told him differently. There was a connection with a beautiful, strange girl, he wagered silently as he climbed into the saddle, turned the pinto westward. Not just curiosity, not just personal satisfaction rode with him now, but a cold anger. He prodded the pinto into a trot and hurried on.

The doubled-over rock was an easy landmark to spot when he reached the area, a strange formation that fitted its name exactly, doubling back upon itself to form a stone arch. He rode beneath it, turned north, had gone another half-mile when he saw the house, a low-roofed, sprawling, unpainted place that looked like an expanded version of a sodbuster's hut. It was set into a small clearing beyond a thick cluster of snowbrush with their masses of tiny white flowers.

Two figures were working on a pump handle outside the house as Fargo brought the pinto to a halt. One figure was very tall, at least six-four, Fargo estimated, and very thin, with a narrow frame that made him look like a misplaced tamarack. The other figure was short, and both were stripped to the waist. But as the two men looked up, Fargo saw they had one thing in common. Both had the vacant half-grins and oafish expressions of the semiretarded dullard. The very tall one blinked, stared at him as a slow frown slid over his long-jawed face. He blinked again and turned his head to the house, shouted in an unexpectedly powerful voice. "*Pa!* Pa, git out here," he called.

Fargo's eyes went to the door of the house, saw the figure appear, an unshaven, beefy-faced man with small eyes, clothed in a torn shirt and overalls. The man stared out at him for a moment, suddenly reached behind the door. Fargo flung himself from the pinto, landed on the ground with both feet as the man's arm returned holding a heavy old carbine. Fargo dived into the snowbrush as the first shot blasted over his head, rolled deeper into the thick brush, and came up with the Colt in hand to fire a quick shot. He saw the man in the doorway leap backward, disappear from view. The two oafs were kneeling on the ground beside the pump handle.

"Toomis," Fargo shouted. "Dammit, I want to talk." He swore under his breath. He was becoming a damn shooting gallery, it seemed. "You hear me in there, Toomis?" he called again, waited, heard no

53

reply. The two figures beside the pump handle stayed motionless. Suddenly he heard a horse snort, saw the animal bolt from behind the house, the over-all-clad figure clinging to its back. "Shit," Fargo muttered. He hadn't expected the man to flee out a back window, and he watched as horse and rider raced up the narrow road and vanished around a bend. He stood up, holstered the Colt. No mistaken identity, he murmured silently, not twice in a row. Moving from the snowbrush, he saw the tall figure get to its feet, the shorter one follow suit, their faces mirroring a dull confusion.

"I take it you're the Toomis boys," Fargo said. Edna's description of them had been highly accurate. They were idiots, or they bordered on it. The very tall one nodded, a slow grin coming over his long-jawed, oafish face.

"I'm Zeke," he said.

"I'm Zach," the shorter one added, adopted the same dull grin.

Fargo stared at the tall one, decided to try to reach behind the strange, almost blank eyes. "What the hell's going on around here?" he asked.

The very tall Toomis brother somehow managed to grin and frown at the same time, and Fargo watched the tall form seem to grow taller as the man opened and closed his hands in slow motion. "I'm going to kill you, mister," Zeke Toomis said.

Fargo heard Zach Toomis laugh, a strange, gurgling sound. "That's right, Zeke. Kill him," Zach chortled.

"Now, why'd you want to do a thing like that?" Fargo asked, keeping his voice calm, almost casual.

"I'm going to do it for Pa," the treelike form said.

"I just want to talk some. I don't want trouble," Fargo said placatingly. The long-jawed face was frowning now. "Let's talk some," Fargo said softly.

"Git him, Zeke," he heard the other one chortle again. "You can break him in half."

"Yep, I can break him in half," the tall one echoed as the grin returned to his face. He took a step toward Fargo and the Trailsman backed a few paces, continued to keep his voice soothing.

"You don't want to do that, Zeke," he said. "I just want some answers. Why'd your pa light out like that just now?"

"He went to git help, but we don't need help," the tall form said.

Fargo watched him start to move toward him again, looking like a half-naked tree, the dull-witted grin fixed on his face. Fargo tried one more time. "Now, Zeke, let's be friends," he said.

"I'm going to break you in half," Zeke Toomis said through the fixed grin.

Fargo took another step backward, swore under his breath. Words didn't penetrate. Maybe pain would snap his dull-witted fixation with killing him and jar him into talking. Fargo went into a half-crouch, his powerful arms half-raised. He was ready for Zeke's rush when it came, and yet it surprised him with its speed. The tall form catapulted itself at him, one long arm whistling out in a powerful swing that Fargo just managed to duck away from, to see Zeke Toomis following through with another rush. Fargo came in under the man's long arms, sent a powerful blow into Zeke's midsection. The vacant grin stayed fixed on Zeke Toomis' face as the man barely paused, drove forward again with another roundhouse swing. Fargo ducked away as the blow whistled over his head, and out of the corner of his eye, he saw Zach Toomis dancing in a half-circle, clapping his hands excitedly.

"Hit him, Zeke. Kill him for Pa," Zach chortled.

Fargo continued to easily avoid the wildly swinging blows aimed at him, waited his chance, set himself flat-footed, and lifted a tremendous blow into Zeke Toomis' ribs. He felt the middle rib bone snap and this time the tall, treelike form stumbled sideways. Fargo drove another blow into the same spot. The grunt of pain carried surprise with it and a slow frown of incomprehension came over the vacant face. A normal person would have sunk down in excruciating pain, but Zeke only stared at the big black-haired man as though he were trying to understand how he'd been hurt. He came in again, arms outstretched, seeking to close them around Fargo's neck. Zeke leaped and Fargo ducked low, again surprised by the man's speed, and brought up a right uppercut. But Zeke was coming in too fast and the blow slid upward along his chest, reaching his chin with a glancing effect, and Fargo twisted his body to the side as Zeke crashed into him. He felt himself toppling sideways, as though a tree had fallen on him. Zeke got one long arm around his neck and yanked backward, but Fargo let his knees buckle, slipped down out of the man's grasp. He spun, delivered another hard blow into the snapped rib bone. Zeke let out a sharper grunt of pain, halted, and Fargo ducked into the clear.

"Hit him, Zeke, git him now," Fargo heard Zach exhort, his voice taking on a disappointed whine. Zeke started forward again, tried to get both arms around his foe as Fargo ducked from a series of wild lunges. A dull stare had come into Zeke's face and Fargo watched him start forward again, swing another long-armed blow. Fargo came in under it, drove a hard left into the snapped rib, and Zeke halted, an expression of pain finally coming into the slow-witted face. Fargo followed with a hard right, all the power of his shoulder and back behind it.

The blow connected exactly at the point of Zeke

Toomis' long jaw and Fargo saw the figure halt, quiver for a moment. He smashed another blow in at once, at the same spot. Zeke took two steps backward, seemed suddenly at a loss, and Fargo drove in two more punches. The tall bean-pole figure swayed and this time Fargo came in with a downward, arched swing that crashed into the side of the long face. Zeke fell to one knee, started to get up, and Fargo smashed his jaw again and Zeke Toomis fell onto both knees, his head hanging down. The dull-witted must also have a dulled threshold of pain, Fargo decided, for most men would have been demolished by now. But Zeke was attempting to get to his feet, and Fargo reared back, delivered another tremendous blow to the man's jaw. Zeke Toomis pitched forward onto his face, taking a few extra seconds to do so, as an extra-tall tree takes longer to fall. He lay there, twitched for a moment, then was still.

Fargo rubbed his right arm and turned to Zach Toomis, who had stopped dancing about and was staring at his brother's prostrate form. Slowly he brought his eyes up to stare at Fargo with the comprehension of a slow eight-year-old. Fargo shot a glance along the narrow road, aware time could run out on him at any moment. He took a step toward Zach Toomis and the man immediately bent away, twisting his body in a submissive position of fear. "Don't hit me," he cried out, whining in anticipated pain.

"Then talk. I want Lisa," Fargo barked.

The dullard began to straighten out, but his face still held the fear of pain in it. "Lisa?" he echoed tentatively.

"Yes, Lisa, goddammit," Fargo roared in frustrated anger. "Christ, don't you know your own sister?"

He saw the grin start to move into Zach Toomis' face. "Sure I know Lisa," he half-gurgled.

"Where the hell is she?" Fargo snapped.

The grin took on another shade, as though he was a child hiding a secret. "Run off," he said.

"Run off? When?" Fargo pressed.

Zach Toomis frowned as he thought back. It was obviously an effort. "Last night," he said slowly. "Yet, it was last night." He shrugged. "I'm not good at countin'," he explained.

"You sure it was last night?" Fargo questioned.

The dullard's brow furrowed again. He nodded slowly. "Last night," he said again. "She come back the day before. I've got it right," he said with defensiveness.

"She run off on foot?" Fargo asked.

"Nope, took the big-footed gelding, she did. Made Pa even madder," Zach said, grinned childlike.

Fargo tried to see behind the half-vacant face, decided it was impossible. "Why'd she run off like that?" he asked, keeping his tone pleasant, as though he were trying to pull information from a child.

"She and Pa had a big fight. He knocked her down," Zach said, grinned again.

Fargo took in the reply and smiled back, aware that answers had to be drawn in bits and pieces from the idiot. "What'd they fight about, Zach?" he asked casually.

"Don't know that." Zach Toomis shrugged.

Fargo cast a glance at the narrow road, decided to risk a moment more. "Why'd Zeke call for your pa when I rode up?" he asked.

"Pa told Zeke and me to tell him if we saw anyone riding a fancy pinto," Zach answered.

"Why?" Fargo pressed quietly.

Zach shrugged again. "He didn't say, just told us to look out for it," he answered.

Fargo peered at the vacant face for a moment more and turned away. There was nothing further to learn from Zach Toomis. He swung onto the pinto, rode around the house to the back, where he saw two more horses hitched to a rail. He leaned from the saddle, his eyes sweeping the soil in long, slow circles. The lake-blue eyes missed nothing, for they were eyes that saw out of the wellspring of experience and the wisdom of instinct, eyes that made the ground into a pageless book, every mark a word, every print a sentence. They were the eyes of the Trailsman.

The fresh imprints of the horse Toomis had raced away were easy to see and discard, and Fargo edged the pinto forward one step at a time, sorting through the array of hoofmarks that covered the ground. He'd reached the rear corner of the house when he picked up the prints of the horse Zach Toomis had called the big-footed gelding and he grunted in satisfaction. The horse wore oversize shoes that would make trailing it that much easier. He was becoming grateful for small favors. Following the tracks, he headed across the narrow road, glanced back and saw Zeke Toomis on his hands and knees, shaking his head back and forth. Fargo moved on, his eyes on the ground where the big-footed tracks led northwest to border the high country.

He'd learned a little more, but too damned little. He was hunted, wanted, dead or alive, it seemed, and beautiful Lisa Toomis had fled her home. They were facts that told him nothing, left the puzzle unanswered. Like the isolated rock projections that rose on a desert plain, they stood unconnected, entirely apart from each other. But there was a connection, and it all still came down to a gorgeous mystery named Lisa. In twenty-four hours she had made him a stud and a shooting gallery and he still hadn't the damnedest idea why. His mouth tightened with anger that was part grudging admiration.

He found his eyes straining to pick up tracks. It was heavily grassed terrain and there'd been enough time for most of the grass to spring back into place. Twice he realized he'd gone wrong, had to retrace steps until he could find another oversize hoofprint. He was grateful when she took a narrow passage that was more dirt than grass. She kept to a line that edged the high country but moved through rolling foothills, plenty of timber, and grassy slopes. It was just past midday when he came onto a small mountain stream. She'd halted there, he saw in the marks at the soft bank, let the horse drink, and then slept beneath the branches of a big bur oak nearby.

He studied the ground beneath the tree, saw that some of the grass and brush was still slowly springing back into place. She hadn't left all that long ago, and he returned to the pinto to hurry on. He gained time as she took a long, narrow pathway that had been worn flat by deer and moose. It made tracking easier, and she wasn't pushing the big-footed gelding, her trail showed, her pace steady as she stayed on the passageway and kept away from open country. Fargo quickened his pace and the afternoon sun was beginning to slide downward when he reined up sharply, the frown digging into his brow. He stared down at the new set of tracks that had suddenly appeared on the narrow pathway, the short-strided, unshod imprints of Indian ponies. Three, Fargo counted, not crossing the pathway but swinging in behind the tracks of the big-footed gelding.

"Damn," Fargo swore softly, his eyes intent on the

ground as he moved forward. The three Indian ponies had definitely taken up following Lisa Toomis, he saw, and he swore again, halted at a soft place where an underground spring moistened the surface soil. He dismounted, ran his hands over the tracks. They were fresh, the edges giving way slowly to the pressure of his fingers. Not more than an hour old, he estimated as he remounted and went forward again.

The tracks stayed the same for almost an hour and Fargo felt the frown deepening on his face. The three Indians had plainly spotted Lisa, but they'd had plenty of time to close in and seize her. Yet they'd only followed, and Fargo, glimpsing a path branching up into the high hills, turned the pinto upward. He sent the horse up the path at a fast trot, leveled off high on the hillside, and moved westward, his lake-blue eyes sweeping the ground below. He'd gone less than a half-mile when his eyes caught the faint movement below, a bush trembling, a tree branch swaying, and he halted, peered down until, through a break in the foliage, he saw the riders appear. The three Indians were riding single file, clothed only in moccasins and breechclouts. One wore an armband and each carried a tomahawk held at the waist by a leather thong.

He was too distant to pick up any tribal marks. He watched the three horsemen move along the narrow path, vanish behind thick trees. He spurred the pinto on, staying on the high ground and moving past the three riders below. Light was fading fast, dusk pulling a gray-purple shroud over the land, and he hurried, eyes straining along the pathway that snaked its way below. And then he spotted her, long, thick black hair unmistakable, hanging to the center of her back. She rode the gelding slowly, obviously unaware she was being followed.

Fargo halted, peered back, and glimpsed the three Indians coming along the path. They continued to follow, hold back, and it wasn't a matter of simple idle interest, he damn well knew. A little icy smile came to brush his lips, and confirmation of his thoughts followed as he watched, saw them halt for a whispered conference, then send the ponies into an instant, effortless gallop to become forms flashing through the trees. They'd decided to move in before the light disappeared, and from his high vantage point Fargo saw Lisa Toomis turn in her saddle as the sound of galloping hooves reached her. He was too far away to see the terror that gripped her beautiful face, but he knew it was there as she sent the gelding bolting forward. It was no contest, the big-footed gelding sure and steady but no speed horse. The fleet Indian ponies caught up with her in moments and Fargo saw the first Indian pull Lisa out of the saddle. The other two were on her as she hit the ground, quickly yanking her to her feet.

Fargo started down from the high ground, quickly losing sight of the three red men and Lisa, not hurrying his descent. There was no need. It'd be dark before he reached the path and the Indians would be in no hurry. They'd settle down, decide how to best enjoy their prize; Fargo's eyes hardened at the thought. He had other ideas about that. No damn trio of wandering Indians was going to cheat him out of the answers only Lisa Toomis could supply. He continued moving down the slope and the dark of night had wrapped itself around the forest as he reached the pathway. He turned on the narrow passage, rode for a few minutes longer, then slid from the saddle to go on foot, the pinto following behind him. He heard their voices first, then glimpsed the tiny fire they'd set. He draped the pinto's reins over a low branch and crept forward on feet soundless as a mountain lion's padded paws. He set down in a crouch as he reached the place where the Indians had made camp between two thick bur oaks.

A rope had been placed around Lisa's neck, the other end held by a short-trunked Indian. Fargo's glance went to the other two, one of medium height with a broad face, the other taller, with long black hair so heavily greased that Fargo could smell the bear fat. He glanced down at their moccasins, saw the figured beadwork of the Shoshoni. As he watched, the tall one moved to stand in front of Lisa, who, even in the dim firelight, was as completely beautiful as he'd remembered, liquid black eyes and patrician nose, her beautifully curved breasts now straining against a green shirt as she stood very straight before the Indian. Fargo watched as the Shoshoni ran his hands across her face, feeling each feature, moved down over her shoulders, then onto her breasts, and Fargo heard his grunting sound of pleasure. It was cut short as Lisa Toomis brought one hand up and tried to rake her nails across his face. He ducked away but not before she'd drawn blood along his cheekbone. The short Shoshoni holding the rope yanked hard and Fargo heard Lisa's gasp of pain as she fell to her knees. She stayed there, one hand rubbing her neck.

The greasy-haired one let out a roar of rage, kicked her in the ribs, and she fell sideways with another gasp of pain. He reached down, tore the shirt open, and the beautiful twin mounds spilled out. This time he ran his hands over both as the other Indian held the rope tight around the girl's neck. Fargo swore under his breath as the Indian pressed the deep, full breasts and laughed, drew his legs up, and straddled the girl, sitting over her hips. He was beginning to make motions with his pelvis, thrusting, unmistakable motions, laughing as he did, and

63

Fargo saw the terror on the girl's face as he lifted his breechclout for her to see, threw his head back in laughter. Fargo, his mouth thin, drew the big Colt. He hadn't wanted gunshots that could draw more trouble. He had it out of the holster when he saw the Shoshoni with the broad face rush forward, barrel into the Indian straddling Lisa Toomis, knocking him to the ground. The tall one leaped to his feet and angry shouts filled the air, the broad-faced one gesticulating wildly.

They spoke a dialect of Shoshonean he didn't know, but it quickly became clear that the argument was about who had first rights to their prize. The broad-faced one suddenly whirled, marched directly toward the brush where Fargo lay, and the Trailsman flattened himself on the ground. He saw the Indian halt only a few feet away, select three long, thin branches, break them to the same length, and return to the others. He thrust the branches into the fire, left the ends protruding, and Fargo rose to one knee again. They were playing a variation of choosing straws. The one whose branch took longest to burn down would be the winner, and Fargo watched as the three Shoshoni gathered to watch the flames begin to catch at the three twigs, Lisa still on the ground, buttoning the few remaining buttons on her shirt.

Fargo holstered the Colt and pushed himself backward. The branches would take a few minutes to burn, more than enough time for him to return to the pinto. He moved back in his long-strided crouching gait, reached the pinto, and drew his double-edged throwing knife from the saddlebag, the kind known as an Arkansas toothpick, thin and long and perfectly balanced. When he returned to the Indians, the tall, greasy-haired Shoshoni was gleefully clapping his hands as his twig burned the longest.

He let out a whoop of satisfaction as the other two twigs burned down, took the rope away from the short one, and pulled Lisa to him. She came half-stumbling, and when he yanked hard at the rope, she went down on her knees. As Fargo watched, the broad-faced one went to his pony and reached into a small deerskin pouch, brought out a long piece of pemmican. He sat down, broke it in three, and handed a piece to each of the other two. The tall one holding Lisa took his, sat down with it, and Fargo saw Lisa frown as she watched the three Shoshoni begin to chew their pemmican in silence.

Fargo grunted inwardly, unsurprised. Indians were realists, the stomach before the loins. Besides, they had plenty of time to enjoy their captive. His eyes narrowed as he measured distances and he turned the thin blade in his hand. The first move would have to be perfect, exactly on target at the right moment. It had to cut the odds by a third and give him that all-important advantage of surprise. He crouched motionless, like a lynx watching a grouse, and saw the tall one finish his dried pemmican and stand up. The Shoshoni yanked hard on the rope and Lisa Toomis stumbled forward. He grabbed a fistful of her long, thick hair and flung her to the ground as she cried out in pain. He was atop her instantly, half-laughing, half-roaring, pinning her flat, starting to push open her writhing legs. He held one forearm over her breasts, keeping her arms back at the same time as he pushed her thighs open with his powerful legs.

Fargo shot a glance at the other two. They were intent on their pemmican, totally ignoring everything else. Lisa gasped in pain and then in fear, her gasp turning into a sobbing cry as the Shoshoni flung her skirt up, let out a roar of anticipation as he pushed between her legs and started to move himself upward. His breechclout was up now and his bronzed buttocks glistened with a faint coat of perspiration, and Fargo smelled the musklike odor of the man, an odor of fish oil and buffalo grease let loose by sexual arousal. Fargo rose up on his feet, his arm going back, the blade poised for an instant longer. Lisa's scream of terror rent the night. The Shoshoni had her legs forced wide, her smooth, milk-white little belly exposed. He lifted himself half up to ram forward. Fargo's arm came down and the slender blade hurtled through the air with such speed it was all but invisible. It hit its mark just as the Shoshoni started to thrust forward.

His body came to an abrupt halt and his neck jerked upward, then back, the grease-laden hair flapping wildly as the thin, doubled-edged blade went all the way through his neck to come out the other side, stopped only by the hilt. The Indian's hands lifted, pawed at his throat as his mouth fell open in soundless gasps. He began to fall sideways as two thin trickles of red started down both sides of his neck. Fargo was through the brush in one silent stride, saw Lisa staring in disbelief at the Shoshoni as he fell and at the knife that had suddenly appeared through his neck as if by magic.

The other two Indians were just lifting their eyes as they heard the tall one fall to the ground. The broad-faced Shoshoni still held a last piece of pemmican in his hand as Fargo came out of the trees like a silent wraith. His eyes widened and he started to get up as Fargo smashed the butt of the Colt down into the center of his forehead and felt the bone crack. The Indian toppled backward, but the third, stocky one had leaped to his feet, the short-handled tomahawk in his hand at once.

The surprise faded from his black eyes, turned to cold fury as he moved in a half-circle. Fargo dropped the Colt into its holster and moved with the red man. He watched the Indian's feet, saw his toes dig into the ground, and gained the split second that let him duck the lunge and the tomahawk that just grazed his head. He tried to get in a counterpunch to the man's midsection, but the Indian was fast, twisted aside, swung the ax again, and Fargo had to give ground. He stepped backward and out of the corner of his eye, he saw Lisa Toomis on her feet, pulling the rope from around her neck. The Shoshoni moved in again and Fargo continued to back, watched the Indian's right foot twist into the ground, and dived in the other direction as the tomahawk whistled past his ear. This time he lifted a tremendous blow, sank it into the Indian's belly, and saw the stocky form double over. Fargo started in with a downward blow, had to dive away as the Indian brought the tomahawk around in a flat circle.

The Shoshoni moved forward and once again Fargo backed, let the Indian come toward him. He feinted a right and the Shoshoni reacted instantly, brought the tomahawk down in a short arc, but Fargo's blow came from the other side, smashing into the man's face. The Indian staggered for a moment, but the moment was enough for Fargo to follow with a driving right that exploded against the side of the man's jaw. The Shoshoni dropped to his knees, but his hand still clutched the tomahawk and Fargo heard the sound of hooves, looked up, to see Lisa racing off on the big-footed gelding. He started to let out an oath, cut it off, and leaped aside as the Indian, from his knees, brought the tomahawk down at his ankle. Fargo felt the edge of the blade graze his shin, whirled, half-jumped, and came down on the Indian's wrist with the end of his heel. He felt the wrist crack and the Shoshoni let out a short cry of pain, tried to turn away, but Fargo's blow smashed downward into his face. He fell backward, Fargo's heel still on his wrist, and Fargo yanked the Colt from its holster, brought the heavy butt end down onto the man's head. The stocky form twitched and then lay still.

Fargo straightened, looked into the dark of the trees. He could still hear the gelding racing through the forest and this time he didn't stop the oath that exploded from his lips. He paused only long enough to retrieve the throwing knife, pulling it free in one quick motion and wiping it clean on the grass. He raced back to the pinto, was in the saddle in moments, turned the horse to go after Lisa Toomis. He let his acute hearing find her, follow her every turn; he heard her as she ran into branches, halted, turned away, tried another direction. She was running blindly in the blackness of the woodland, just hoping to get away, and he continued to track her by sound, avoided low-hanging branches himself, skirted thick clusters of shrubs. She was trying to hurry where hurrying was impossible, and she was paying the price. He caught up to her quickly, came upon her as she was pulling back from a clump of entangling buckthorn, her hair in disarray, a long scratch across her neck. She saw him, reined up, stared at him as he came up to halt in front of her.

"I said till next time," Fargo half-whispered. "Next time is here."

Disarrayed, disheveled, she was still a beautiful creature and the black liquid eyes suddenly held the weariness of defeat. "It won't help you," she said, and he frowned. "Your chasing after me," she continued. "Why did you do it?"

"You forgot to answer some questions," he said. "And I don't like being a shooting gallery. I'm funny that way." Her lips tightened. "You're lucky I came looking," he told her. "If I hadn't, you'd be dead, or wish you were, come tomorrow." She swallowed, but he thought he caught the flicker of admission in the black orbs. "Those Shoshoni followed you for at least two hours," he said.

Surprise crossed her face. "Why'd they hold off so long?" she asked.

Fargo uttered a short, harsh laugh. "They couldn't figure you, a beautiful white girl, riding alone up here. They were afraid you were some kind of decoy. They followed until they were sure you weren't the bait for a trap." He turned the pinto, motioned to her to follow. "This way," he muttered.

"Where are you going?" she asked.

"You've got a lot of answering to do. I want to make camp first," he growled as she swung the gelding alongside the pinto's rump. He led the way through the timberland until it thinned and he found a rock overhang that formed a natural roof and a protected place. He dismounted, watched her get off the gelding, and tethered her horse beside the pinto. As he got a small fire started, she took a canvas sack from behind the gelding's saddle, fished a brush out, and used it on her hair.

"When'd you eat last?" he asked as he took some beef jerky from his saddlebag, warmed it over the small fire.

"You've no need to feel sorry for me," she returned.

"I'm not. Just answer the question," he growled.

"Two days back," she muttered, and he handed her one of the strips of jerky, watched her take it and waste no time biting into it. He leaned against the stone wall at his back and ate his strip. Only two buttons were left to hold her shirt together and her full, deep breasts rose beautifully from the open neckline. She saw him admiring the view, tried to pull the shirt together.

"You got a bad memory?" he asked, and her frown was questioning. "It's a little late for getting modest," he finished.

"That was different," she flared.

"Not so's I can see," Fargo said.

"I don't expect you'd understand. How'd you find me?" she asked.

"I'm good at it," he said.

"Yes, the Trailsman," she muttered.

"Only you didn't believe I'd come looking," Fargo speared, saw her round black eyes glance away. "Or was it that you didn't expect I'd be alive long enough to come looking?" he said, caught the tiny tightening at the corners of her lovely lips.

She half-shrugged. "Does it really matter?" she asked with sudden weariness.

"It sure as hell matters to me," Fargo barked. "I've been tricked, drugged, used, shot at, and had to fight three Shoshoni. Now I want those goddamn answers you owe me. You can give them to me all nice and easy or black-and-blue."

She glowered at him for a long moment. "I had to do it," she said sullenly, and still managed to look beautiful.

"I've heard that excuse used for a lot of things," Fargo said coldly.

"Pa Toomis *sold* me," she flung at him with sudden fury.

It was Fargo's turn to frown. "Your pa sold you?"

"He's not my pa," the girl snapped back. "I'm known as Lisa Toomis to folks, but my name's Lisa Brewer. My real folks died of the fever when I was eleven. Toomis took me in. It wasn't just goodness. I know that now. He needed someone to help around his place besides those two idiot sons of his. But he saw other uses for me as I grew up."

"And beautiful," Fargo added. "That explains one thing I wondered about."

"Which was?"

"How you and those two retards could come out of the same stud farm," Fargo said. "So Toomis sold you. How did I come to fit in anywhere?"

He saw Lisa's mouth tighten for a moment. "He sold me to Bart Bullmer for a thousand dollars because I was a virgin and Bart Bullmer only takes virgins," Lisa said. "But he's a monster—Big Bart they call him—and a girl is lucky to last a year with him. I heard of one girl who killed herself because she couldn't stand it any longer and they say he killed two others after a year because he got tired of them. From what I've heard tell about Bart Bullmer, they were better off dead." She paused, took in a deep breath, and the two buttons almost lost their battle to keep her modest. "But I knew one thing," she continued. "He wouldn't have me if I weren't a virgin anymore, even though he'd had his eye on me for years. That's the way he is."

Fargo's lake-blue eyes narrowed at her. It was half an answer, one that still skirted the heart of it. "Seems to me all a gal like you would need to do was wave a finger at any of the local boys," he slid at her.

The black orbs met the hardness in his stare. "None of them would touch me, bad as they all wanted to," she said.

"Why not?" he snapped.

She took a moment before answering. "Because they knew it'd be like signing their own death warrant," she said. "They knew Bart Bullmer would kill the man who did it if he had to turn the territory inside out to find him. They wouldn't have touched me even at gunpoint, none of them."

Fargo felt his simmering anger rising to a boil. "So

you had to find a stranger, somebody you could set up as a fall guy," he exploded. "You used me as a tool and a target." Lisa's silence was the silence of admission. "Damn, I was perfect for you. Enough people know me and I've an Ovaro that's rare and easy to spot." She nodded and had enough conscience to look uncomfortable as his eyes blazed into her. "You're an all-fired little bitch, aren't you?" he flung at her.

He saw protest flare in the black eyes. "There was no other way for me, no other way," she returned.

"You're good at giving yourself excuses, too. You're as rotten as you are beautiful," he answered.

"You call it rotten. I call it something else," she said, angry defensiveness in her voice.

"Such as?" Fargo pressed.

"Surviving," she said. He uttered a sharp noise that drew an angry glare from her. "You can't understand," she said.

"I know about surviving, too damn much about it," he told her.

"Not this kind. You can't understand it because you've never known what it's like to be absolutely helpless. A man, especially one like you, can fight back, do *something*, maybe have some kind of chance. I'd no chance at all against Bart Bullmer. I couldn't stand up to him. I couldn't fight, reason, run. I couldn't even beg. He'd only enjoy that most of all. There was nothing else for me, no other way. I had to do the only thing that'd make him turn away from me."

"Those are all hiding-place words," Fargo threw back, and saw her almost wince. "You figured to trade somebody else's neck for your own—mine, as it turned out—and that still spells rotten. There's right and there's wrong, whether you're big or small, strong or weak."

72

He saw the liquid black eyes blink and she looked away and her voice was suddenly very small. "I never said it was right," she murmured.

"You're just trying to give it a face that'll let you live with yourself," he snapped. Her lips pressed tightly together and she made no reply. "Those four cowhands, how come they agreed to help you?" Fargo asked.

"They weren't from around here. I paid them plenty and they ran as soon as they'd done their job," Lisa said.

"Where'd you get the money to pay them and Edna Corrigan?" he questioned, saw the surprise touch her face.

"My folks left me a little when they died. I used all of it for this," she said.

"And when it was finished, you went home to Toomis and told him you weren't a virgin anymore," Fargo said. "You told him a man called the Trailsman, who rides an Ovaro, had taken you."

"Yes," she said, her voice small, her eyes turned away.

"That's when you had the fight with him and he hurried off to tell this Big Bart," Fargo pressed, and she nodded.

"I didn't want to do it, not any of it," she said, emphasizing the last words.

"You said that," Fargo answered harshly as he studied her. It had all come together to make a grim kind of sense now, from the way she'd acted in bed that day to the gunslingers who had started blasting the minute they saw him. "What now?" he asked almost casually.

She half-shrugged. "I keep going," she said.

"Guess again," Fargo growled.

He watched her eyes go to him, a frown starting

73

to slide across the smoothness of her forehead. "What does that mean?" she asked.

"My neck's still on the line," Fargo bit out.

The frown gathered apprehension and she tried a quick answer for him. "Maybe not. Maybe he's called off looking for you."

Fargo half-sprang forward and his fist slammed down onto the ground. "Like hell he has, and you know better. No more sweet-talking bullshit from your beautiful lips, you hear me?" he thundered.

She swallowed, a moment of fear in her black eyes, found her voice. "All right, I'm sorry. No, he hasn't called off looking for you. He won't till he finds you. By now every drifter knows that Big Bart wants the Trailsman, the man on the Ovaro. I'm sure he's offered plenty for your hide. All you can do is run."

"Run, and sooner or later you get caught. Besides, I don't like looking over my shoulder. I've got a better idea," Fargo said, drawing a frown from her. "You and me, we're going calling," he said. The frown became gathering horror and her lips opened in soundless protest. "You're going to take me off the hook, sweetie. You'll tell him you set it all up yourself."

"No, oh, no. It's impossible," she said, finding her voice. "It can't work."

"I'll see that he doesn't touch you. I just want him off my tail. All you have to do is speak your piece," Fargo said.

"He won't listen and he won't care. He's a madman, a monster," Lisa said. "He'll kill you no matter what I say."

"Glad to see you've become so concerned over my neck all of a sudden," Fargo slid at her, and her eyes flashed.

"All right, I'm being selfish. Is that what you want me to say?" she thrust at him.

He half-shrugged. "A little honesty helps," he said.

"Now I've said it and it doesn't change anything. Bart Bullmer will kill you anyway," she insisted.

"I figure the truth is always worth a try," Fargo told her, saw her lips bite down on each other. "Now I'm going to get some sleep. You got a blanket in that sack of yours?" he asked.

She shook her head. "Just a big shawl. That's all I had time to take, besides some clothes," she said. "I used it last night."

"Froze your little ass off, too, I'll wager," Fargo said.

"I can make do with it again tonight," she said, brushing aside the truth of his words.

"You'll sleep in my bedroll tonight," he said.

"I will not," she bristled. "Don't get any ideas because of the other afternoon. That was different."

"I know, that was strictly sacrifice," he slid at her.

Her chin lifted. "That's a good-enough word for it," she said.

"No matter, you sleep in my bedroll next to me or I tie you up. I just want you where I can get some sleep, nothing else," he said.

She tossed him a frown of skepticism. "Nothing else?"

"You heard me," he growled.

The skepticism stayed in her eyes. "That's not like you, from what I've heard," she said.

"You can count on it tonight," he told her.

The frown took on something more than skepticism, a hint of very female curiosity. "Why?" she questioned.

"I figure I've already done enough for you," Fargo said blandly, saw her mouth come open for an instant, then clamp shut. She rose, went to the canvas sack, and took out a flannel nightdress, went behind the gelding. Fargo laid out the bedroll and blanket as he let the fire burn down to but a few embers. He undressed to his shorts, the Colt in its holster beside the bedroll, stretched out, and waited. When she stepped out from behind the gelding she had a nightdress on, dark blue, hanging to her feet, a scooped neckline. It hung loose but not loose enough to hide the deep swell of her breasts or the soft curve of her hips. The few embers caught her in a faint glow, the long black hair moving gently in the night wind, no ordinary girl in a flannel nightdress but a startlingly beautiful wraith out of the night.

She halted and Fargo saw her eyes flick across the muscled beauty of his body as he lay stretched out on the bedroll, pass over the bulge that marked his maleness. Tiny lines deepened at the corners of her mouth as she took her eyes from him, sank down on the bedroll, turned her back to him, her legs drawn up. He pulled the blanket over them, smelled the faint odor of her, muskily female, the lingering traces of powder still with her. He stretched out on his back and she stayed at the very edge of the bedroll, leaving a wall of airspace between them.

"Now, isn't this much cozier than being hog-tied?" he asked casually.

"Good night," she muttered stiffly.

She couldn't see Fargo smile into the dark as he closed his eyes. Beautiful Lisa may have put him into a hornet's nest, but he'd get a taste of honey before he was through.

She slept soundly, stirring only once, causing him to
wake instantly. He watched her turn, sigh, just the
edge of her face visible behind the curtain of jet
hair. When the first sun sent yellow streaks through
the trees, he woke, rose, his nostrils catching the
scent at once on the morning wind, a fresh, clean
scent. He'd just drawn on trousers when he heard
her wake and sit up, long thick hair forming a jet
halo around her face and her black liquid eyes
quickly shaking away sleep. She rose, each movement graceful, even in the shapeless flannel
nightdress.

"There's a stream near, just past those trees, I'd
guess," Fargo said.

"A stream. Wonderful," Lisa said, smiling. "You
can go first."

"And leave you here alone?" Fargo smiled back.

"I won't run away," she said.

"I know you won't because we'll go together," he
told her.

"I'm not going to bathe with you there." She
frowned.

"Then you can just watch me, but you're coming
along," Fargo barked, and she glared at him as he
took a bar of hog-fat soap from his saddlebag. She

followed angrily as he started through the trees, the stream coming into sight in a few minutes, deeper and wider than many mountain streams and obviously fed by a waterfall not too far away. She halted at the edge of the stream, her eyes on the cool, clear water. Fargo shed his trousers, pulled off his shorts, stepped into the stream, sank down in the refreshing water, and started to soap himself. He paused for a moment to glance at her.

"Suit yourself, but I'm washing, not watching," he said.

"Damn you, Fargo," he heard her snap as she flung the nightgown off and stepped into the stream, a few feet away, keeping her back to him. The waist-length, thick black hair almost formed a modest covering, but he glimpsed the lovely roundness of her rear as she sank down into the water. She kept her back to him, scooped up handfuls of the bubbling water that flowed past her.

"Soap's coming down," he called, and let the soap out of his hand, watched it rush downstream. She half-turned, reached out to catch it, and he saw the side of one upturned breast gracefully dip as she caught the soap, turned her back once again. He finished rinsing himself, rose, and stepped from the stream into a square of warm sun. He stretched out, watched Lisa as she cast a quick, angry glance back at him.

"You just going to stare?" she snapped.

"Yep," he said.

"Haven't you any sense of decency at all?" she flung back.

"Sure, but I never let it get in the way of enjoying myself," he said mildly.

She turned away, tossed water over herself, and reached out to pull the nightdress to her as she stood up, allowing him only the briefest glance, a flash of full-bodied loveliness. Holding the night-dress in front of her, she found her own square of sun and sank down in it, using the nightdress effectively as she tossed him a quick glare. Fargo laughed, lay back and let the warm sun dry his skin, and finally rose to pull on shorts and trousers. Lisa kept her face determinedly away from him, he saw.

"You ready?" he asked. Her answer was to pull the nightgown over her, get up, and follow him back to where they had camped. She went behind the gelding to change, and he'd just put away the bed-roll and finished dressing when she emerged in a lemon-yellow shirt and black riding skirt. He watched her climb onto the gelding, the lemon shirt pulling tight to outline her breasts, a perfectly smooth roundness, and he remembered how tiny the pink points had been. He smiled inwardly as she continued to look angry. It added a sultriness to her beauty and he swung onto the pinto.

"Where do I find Bart Bullmer?" he asked, saw her hesitate, a hint of slyness coming into her face. "Don't get cute," he warned. "Play ball or you'll ride until your little ass falls off."

Her lips tightened. "All right, he's up in the foothills. You have to cross a narrow river. It's called the Marshhill River because it's half marshland," Lisa said. "You go north from here."

Fargo swung the pinto north, let Lisa bring the big-footed gelding up alongside him. "What's Bart Bullmer do up here besides buy virgins?" he asked.

"He runs a logging operation and hires a lot of men nobody else'd hire," she said, fell silent as he nodded and led the way to the end of the timber-land. She rode in silence for half an hour and sud-denly blurted out the words that had been simmering inside her. "This is crazy, plain crazy.

79

You won't even reach him alive," she said. "No telling how many hands he's got out looking for you."

"That's my problem. All you have to do is tell the truth," Fargo answered, followed a slope of land that led down into a narrow passageway, not wide enough to be called a valley, not narrow enough to be a ravine. Thick brush covered the ground and the sides rose steeply, one side mostly stone with vines running up and down, snaking out of almost every crevice. Fargo steered a course along the center of the passageway and a frown came to his brow as his eyes scanned the brush cover underfoot. The frown stayed, deepened as he picked up sounds, movements, and he saw the gelding begin to swing his rump sideways, nervously blow air. Lisa pulled on the horse's reins, fought his sudden nervousness.

"Keep him in tight," Fargo said sharply. He felt the Ovaro try to speed up, and he stroked the gleaming black hide alongside the neck. "Easy, easy now," he soothed.

Lisa fought the gelding again as the horse half-reared. "Dammit, what's wrong with him?" she asked.

"Horse sense," Fargo said tightly.

"What's that mean?" She frowned.

"This area is a bed of rattlers. The horses have picked it up and they're nervous," he said.

Lisa's black eyes grew wide in instant fright. "How do you know?" she questioned.

"I've been hearing them moving all around us. There's a particular sound snakes make when they move quickly through dry brush," he answered.

"How do you know they're rattlers?" she pressed, holding the gelding in sharply as he snorted again.

"Terrain, behavior, numbers," Fargo said. "This is their kind of country and rattlers congregate a lot more than most snakes. They'll take over an entire area. They're also more nervous than most snakes, more nervous and quicker to react."

"Oh, God," Lisa breathed, and he saw her swallow hard.

"Hold your horse steady," Fargo said quietly. "Keep him in. Just move on steady. No sudden moves and there'll be no trouble." He stroked the pinto's neck again, reached out and put a hand on the gelding—a steady, calm pressure just above the withers—and felt the horse calm at his touch. He moved on another fifty yards and drew a deep breath, saw Lisa was still stiff with fear. "Relax. I think we're out of it," he said.

"You *think*," she echoed unhappily.

"My horse thinks so, too. He's calmed down. That's good enough for me," he said. He let his eyes move up along the vine-covered stone wall, rode a few yards on, and suddenly reined up, the frown on his brow again. He put a finger to his lips in a gesture of silence and Lisa leaned from her saddle.

"What is it?" she whispered. "More rattlers? I didn't hear anything."

"I did," Fargo whispered back, his head tilted to one side, ears straining, and then he heard it again, the creak of stirrup leather, the soft rattle of rein chains. "Riders, on the other side," he said softly, and swung from the pinto. "You stay here," he said.

"No," she said. "I'm not staying here alone."

"I'm just going to have a look," he muttered, began to pull himself up by the vines. The first one broke off in his hand and he tested another carefully before putting his weight on it. He felt it hold, started to climb, using his feet to find crevices for a toehold. He found he had to test each vine as another gave way and he climbed slowly, carefully, the stone facing growing steeper. He was glad it was not really high up to the top as the knuckles of both hands grew red from scraping along the stone where the vines grew tight to the facing. He finally reached the top, got one hand over the edge, and pulled himself up enough to peer over. The stone fell away less sharply on the other side and he saw the six riders moving down a slope below. No passing rangehands, not up here, not one wearing chaps, and they were strung out in twos, riding slowly, scanning the terrain, searching with their eyes.

He was just about to start to lower himself down when he heard the short half-scream. He glanced down to see Lisa half-falling, half-sliding down the side of stone as a vine gave way where she'd started to climb up after him. His eyes snapped to the riders, saw them rein up as one. Damn, he swore under his breath. He wasn't the only one who'd heard her. He let himself slide fast, his hands clinging to the vines as he slid and scraped his way down. The last length of vine gave way as he neared the bottom, and he fell the remaining distance, landing hard on his heels, dropping to one knee as the shock traveled up through his legs. Lisa was just pulling herself to her feet, brushing the long black hair from her face.

"I told you to wait, goddammit," he hissed at her. Her answer was cut off by the sound of the shots, two, evenly spaced, a signal.

"Shit," Fargo swore.

"How many were there?" Lisa asked almost apologetically.

"Six, but there'll be more damn soon," Fargo snapped. "You know, if I didn't need your neck I'd wring it."

"I'm sorry," she offered.

"Get on your damn horse," he rasped as he swung up on the pinto. "*Ride!*" he barked as he sent the pinto racing forward. The land rose, broadened,

82

came to an end as a thinly timbered slope, and he looked behind to find the six riders. They were still a good distance back and to the right, but as he glanced back, he saw another six horsemen appear from around a hill, racing to join up with the first six. Fargo's mouth tightened again as he bent low in the saddle, sent the pinto racing. Lisa rode well enough, he saw, but he found himself cursing as he had to hold back to keep the pinto with the heavy-footed gelding.

The dozen riders had spotted them now, and glancing back, Fargo saw them swerve to give chase. Fargo led the way out of the timber onto a clear stretch. The pursuers had split into two groups, forming a flanking pattern, and Fargo swore again. The damn gelding hadn't speed enough to let him turn, dodge, cut to the side, try to outmaneuver his pursuers. The horse was like an anchor, keeping him and the pinto from making the fast, evasive moves that might give them a chance. He'd no choice but to keep racing straight on, and he glanced back at Lisa, a length behind him, her breasts bouncing with the big-footed gelding's heavy tread. The two groups of riders were staying in position as they gained ground, continuing to outflank him.

Fargo saw a stretch of land dip sharply, headed for it to take the advantage the downhill would give the gelding. The dip quickly became a steady path downhill, and glancing back, he saw four of the pursuers leave the others and swing in behind him as the other two groups stayed on the high ground. He turned his eyes forward as the dip became a funnel that continued downhill as it narrowed, the sides rising up, and he raced into it and instantly felt the land grow softer under the pinto's racing hooves. The two main groups of his pursuers were out of sight now on the high ground and Fargo swore under his breath as realization dawned on him. The ground continued to soften, the pinto's hooves digging in deeper with each stride and the funnel of land leveled. Wild millet, cut-grass, and smartweed came into sight and a harsh sound escaped his lips at the sight of the plants, all marsh growths. A tall line of bay laurel, sandbar willow, and nightshade rose up in front of him to confirm his thoughts.

"That Marshhill River, I think it's just ahead of us," he called to Lisa. "And I think we've got ourselves boxed in."

He reined the pinto to a halt as Lisa came up. He could smell the musky odor of marsh growth now as he slid from the saddle. He didn't need to see his pursuers to know where they were. The two main groups raced along the high ground on both sides of the funnel, most likely on past him by now, and the four others had reined up back at the entrance to the funnel of land.

Lisa, her breath returning, peered anxiously at his tight-lipped handsomeness. "What now?" she asked.

"I'm going on foot to have a look," he said. "If I'm right, that river will be just beyond that wall of trees and nightshade.

"I'm going with you," she said.

"No noise, dammit," he growled, and she nodded, managed to look contrite. He moved forward at his long-strided, crouching lope, wolflike, moving stealthily through the tall weedy aquatic brush. Lisa quickly fell behind and Fargo slipped forward, not waiting for her, ducked under the heavy foliage of the willows, made his way through a dense growth of white vervain. He could feel the moistness of the ground under his feet and the musky marsh odor was strong now. Just past the next growth of sandbar willows he glimpsed the river, water flowing slowly past the end of the funnel of land, the bank heavily overgrown with round-stemmed bulrushes. The river earned its name, he saw, for the water was heavily grown with spike rush and pondweed.

But his gaze took in more than the heavy marsh growth. Eight horsemen had reached the other side of the river, were dismounting, moving along the far bank to face the spot where the funnel of land opened onto the bank, and he hid in the tall marsh grass. Lisa arrived, dropped to her knees beside him, followed his gaze across the slow-moving river. "Bart Bullmer's men. I recognize some of them, the tall one and the one with the bandanna. His name's Ezzner. He's a convicted horse thief."

"Is Bullmer there?" Fargo asked.

She took a moment to scan the men again. "No," she said. "What are they doing?"

"Settling in," Fargo said grimly.

"Why don't they just come across after us?" she asked.

"And get shot up for it?" Fargo returned. "They know we can't cross anywhere else but here. It's the only way out for us."

"What if we go back?" she asked.

"There are four sealing off the other end. They'd nail us before we could get to them there," Fargo said.

"Then we are trapped," she said, defeat flattening her voice.

Fargo's eyes were agate blue as they swept the other bank, moved to the river and its marsh growths. "A trap's no good till it traps something," he muttered, making a mental map of the marshes that rose out of the hardly moving river.

"What are you thinking?" Lisa questioned, quick to grasp at hope.

"We wait for night, first," he said.

She frowned. "Even at night they'll be able to see

us the minute we move out," she said. "They're right across from us. We'd have to ride right into them."

"Maybe," Fargo said, started to slide his way back through the tall grasses. She followed as he led the way back to where they'd left the horses. He sat down against the trunk of a willow.

"What does maybe mean?" she questioned, settling down near him.

"Just what it says," he answered.

"Dammit, Fargo, you could at least tell me what you're thinking," she demanded.

"I'm thinking you ask too many questions," he said.

She glared. "I told you you'd never get the chance to make Bart Bullmer listen," she said.

"If I can reach him my way, he'll listen," Fargo said, closing his eyes.

"What are you going to do?" she asked in exasperation.

"Sleep some," he murmured.

"*Sleep?*" she almost shouted.

"Got any better offers?" he asked, opening his eyes.

"Very funny," she snapped. "We're trapped by men waiting to kill us and you're going to sleep? What are you made out of?"

"Sugar and spice and all kinds of vice," he said. "Now shut up and get some sleep, too. You might need the extra energy come night."

"Night, day, what's the difference? They can't miss seeing us if we try to get out," she said, despondency filling her voice again.

Fargo kept his eyes closed. "They'll waste more bullets at night," he muttered, folded his hands across his midsection, and settled himself comfortably. He heard her move restlessly, finally sit back and grow silent. He let himself lay absolutely still,

86

every muscle relaxing, separating the body and the senses until he slept as a cat does, asleep and yet awake, the body completely at rest and the senses completely awake. No learned skill, though he had worked to bring it to perfection, but a part of him that was in tune with all things wild.

The change in the touch of the wind on his face told him when the night came, but he continued to sleep, letting himself wake only when the moon was rising high in the black velvet of the night sky. Lisa sat straight, he saw, her lovely face milk-white against the long jet hair and the dark of the night. He stretched, got to his feet, reached a hand out to her. She took it and he pulled her to her feet. "It's time," he said.

"Time for what?" she asked, the flatness still in her voice.

"Time to make things happen," he told her, turned, and began to lead the pinto slowly through the willow leaves and the nightshade. "Take the gelding and follow me," he said.

He moved carefully through the foliage and the blackness enveloped him almost at once. Not until he reached the last line of willows almost at the riverbank did the moon filter through the denseness of the leaves. He halted at the edge of the willows. Only the tall grasses lay between him and the river now, and Lisa's shoulder touched his as she halted beside him. He peered through the wan light of the half-moon. Two guards, perhaps fifteen yards apart, stood at the edge of the riverbank, watching, each holding a rifle. The others were back farther, stretched out asleep.

"They're likely doing two-hour shifts. That way everybody gets some shut-eye and stays fresh," Fargo said.

"And they can spot us the minute we move out and wake the rest," she said.

"Not if those two can't see or hear," Fargo murmured, felt her eyes turning to him.

"You couldn't get away with it. They'd see you coming," she said, but he heard the hope curled inside her words.

"Not if I do it right," Fargo said, and his eyes swept the marshy river again, picked out the thick bed of wild rice he had noted earlier. Tall and plume-topped, it rose from the water and grew to the edge of the far bank. The plumed fronds at the top formed a dense curtain that'd be more than ample cover. "You stay here with the horses until I come back. Then you move out with them. Don't swim, just slide into the water with them, let the current carry you downriver. It's not much of a current, but it'll have to do," Fargo told the girl.

"What if you don't come back?" she asked.

"Then you're on your own, honey," he said.

"Thanks a lot," she said, sniffing. "I wouldn't be here if you hadn't dragged me along."

"That makes us even, then, doesn't it?" Fargo returned, and she lowered her eyes, her voice almost inaudible.

"I guess so," she murmured.

"Keep the faith," he said, started to crawl forward through the line of marsh grass, slid into the river as though he were a crocodile leaving its bank. The water was warm and brackish and he kept his arms beneath the surface, pushed himself forward in dog-paddle fashion to move noiselessly through the water. He skirted a bed of pondweed, only the top of his head above the surface of the water, his eyes sweeping the two sentries. They hadn't moved and he continued on, edging a growth of bulrushes, headed for the wild rice. When he reached the edge of it, he halted, treaded water. He was too close for mistakes now. A splash, a sudden ripple of the still water, and the two sentries would hear it, snap alert instantly. He stayed in place, waited until a puff of night breeze rustled the plume-topped wild rice. He moved forward with the soft sound, halted as the reeds grew still again, waited till another puff of wind came to let him swim on for another moment. With the patience of a nighthawk, he waited, moved forward only when the wind rustled the plumed wild-rice reeds.

It was slow, painfully slow, but finally he felt his feet touch the softness of bottom mud. Once more, under cover of a gust of night breeze, he made his way forward, reached the bank where the wild rice halted and shore grass took over, tall enough to hide in if he kept on his stomach. Carefully he began to inch his way forward, his eyes on the nearest sentry, a shadowy figure through the grass. As he drew closer, the man took on defined shape, the rifle still in his hands, his eyes fixed on the far bank across the river. Fargo looked past him to the other sentry, measuring distances. He was closer to the other man than it had seemed from across the river, too close, the Trailsman decided. He'd have to reverse his plans, hit the farthest one first. There'd be no second chance, no room for a mistake. There was room only for a split-second timing and unfailing accuracy. One outcry from either of the two sentries and it'd all blow up in his face. He inched closer on his belly, his hand moving to the double-edged Arkansas toothpick in its sheath. He started to lift himself up on one knee, eyes just above the tops of the marsh grass, when he heard the sound: footsteps, then voices, muttered words first, then words loud and clear.

"Taking over, Sam. Get yourself some shut-eye,"

the voice called, and Fargo saw the two men walking to the bank where the sentries waited. He dropped flat in the tall grass, his face pressed tight against the soft ground. Shit, he swore in silent fury. They were changing shifts. He wanted to curse Lady Luck, decided to thank her instead. If he'd made his move he'd have been caught right in the middle. He heard the men exchange a few words more.

"No sign of 'em yet?" the one asked.

"Nothin'," one of the departing sentries answered.

The other man, a deep, gruff voice, uttered a harsh laugh. "They'll make their move sooner or later. All we've got to do is wait," he said.

Fargo, his face to the ground, listened as the two new sentries settled themselves, stayed motionless until silence took over the riverbank once again. Slowly he lifted his head, peered forward. The two new sentries had taken up almost exactly the same positions as the first two, and a moment of grim satisfaction touched his lips. His plan held, the farthest one first. But not for at least an hour, he swore softly. The two new sentries were far too alert now. He had to let time work on them, dull their sharpness, let them settle down, grow relaxed. He didn't need much, just that moment's jump on them, that split-second edge, but without it, he'd fail. Winning and losing, living and dying, it all came down to split seconds in this land, he reflected as he lay silently.

He settled down in the marsh grass, began to count away the minutes, which seemd like hours. It wasn't long before he felt the tightness gathering inside him, the urge to throw aside waiting and act. Impatience, he grunted to himself. Impatience was the Judas sheep of the emotions. It taunted, urged, prodded, and led the way to death at the most and to mistakes at the least. Past lessons that were seared inside him, and he lay unmoving, breathed in the musky marsh odors. He listened to the deep rumble of a bullfrog's distant call, the soft sound of whirligig beetles, the brushing hiss of the bulrushes as the night wind weaved its way through them. Nearly an hour had gone by when he heard one of the men light a cigarette, and a hard smile crossed his lips. It was a good sign. They were getting bored, relaxing, that edge of alertness gone now.

But he continued to wait until finally his head lifted, and pressing his palms flat into the moist soil, he pushed himself up. The two sentries hadn't shifted positions, their faces still turned to the dark river and the distant bank. But he saw the slump of shoulders, the casual angle of a leg, the rifles held loosely. It was time.

He reached into a shirt pocket and took out a length of thin rawhide, the thongs the Indians used to fringe their ceremonial dress. He always carried a half-dozen in his saddlebag. They came in handy for many things, and now he'd found still another use for them. He wrapped the thong around one finger on his left hand, let it hang loosely as he drew the throwing knife from its sheath. He moved an inch to his left, giving himself a clear line to the farthest sentry. His arm rose, drew back, and his eyes narrowed to near-closed slits measuring distance, trajectory, wind. He paused for that final instant when mind and eye are transferred to muscle control and skill. His arm moved forward with startling speed and the thin blade hurtled through the dark behind the nearest sentry. It cleaved the air in just a trace of shallow arc, hurtling ever so slightly downward as it reached its target and plunged into the man's neck at the base. The double-edged blade drove down through the bottom neck muscles and into the windpipe, halting only when the hilt prevented it from going deeper.

The man simply crumpled to the ground. But Fargo had the thin leather thong stretched tight in both hands before the man touched the ground, leaped forward on soundless cat's feet. As the man crumpled, the nearest sentry turned to him, stared for a moment, frowned. It was enough, that split-second advantage Fargo had waited to achieve. As the sentry began to react, the length of rawhide thong snapped around his throat, pulled tight, instantly shutting off all chance of a sound. Fargo twisted the garrote tighter and the man's hands came up and feebly clawed at the air, the rifle falling to the soft ground, but breath and strength were already denied him. His arms fell limply to his sides as Fargo continued the deadly pressure until he felt the sentry's body sag.

He lowered the still form to the ground, stayed on one knee as his eyes swept the sleeping figures a few yards back from the river's edge. He thought about retrieving his throwing blade, decided it would be pushing his luck. He turned to the dark river at his elbow, lowered himself into the water without causing the sound of a ripple, and began to paddle noiselessly for the opposite shore. He moved in a straight line this time, disdaining the pondweed beds until he reached the other bank, half-rose from the water, and waited. Lisa appeared quickly, leading the two horses, and he saw her eyes were round and still full of apprehension, and he waved at her. She came on, moved into the water, and he met her as the water reached her waist, took the pinto from her.

He held the horse by the cheek strap and floated close alongside him, let the slow river current start to carry him along. Lisa watched, did the same with

92

the gelding, and Fargo slowly turned the pinto in the water as they drifted. The river moved with maddening slowness and Fargo kept one eye on the opposite bank. If someone woke, discovered the sentries, they'd be sitting ducks yet, but he didn't dare push the horses into swimming. The sound would certainly wake someone. He steered through a path of open water between two long beds of pondweed, gratefully felt the river current pick up slightly. He drew a deep breath only when they'd reached a slow bend, the river growing less marsh-filled and the current stronger.

He guided the pinto in a slow half-circle near Lisa and the gelding, spied a break in the thick trees that edged the far bank, and headed for it. "Head for shore," he half-whispered to Lisa, the first words he'd spoken since she entered the river. He reached the shore and pulled himself from the water, the pinto following. He waited for Lisa to come out with the gelding and he climbed into the saddle as water squished from his clothes. Lisa pulled herself onto the gelding, the lemon blouse clinging to her as a wet leaf clings to a stone, molding every line of her breasts, outlining the tiny little points. Her hair hung heavily, wet and glistening, and she was made into still another kind of beauty.

He pulled his eyes away, turned the pinto, and started climbing into the deep of the hills as the moon began to slide across the night sky. He continued upward, pausing at a turn in the path, and Lisa caught up to him. "I'm freezing," she said through teeth that chattered, and he felt the coldness of his own body.

"Hang in a little longer," he told her, and continued on upward into the terrain he was certain would hold caves or deep, covered rock formations. He proved right as they began to pass small black openings in the rocks and mountain timber. He finally halted before one large enough to take in the horses, came down from the saddle, and picked up a piece of wood. He flung it into the cave and listened, ears straining for a sound, a growl, movement, the scrape of claws. He tossed in a second piece, listened again. Finally satisfied that the cave was empty, he entered with the pinto, beckoned Lisa to follow. "It's big enough for us inside," he told her.

"How do you know? It's too dark to see in here," she said.

"It's not too dark to smell," Fargo said.

"How can you smell whether it's big or little?" Lisa frowned.

"A small cave has a sharp, acrid staleness to it. It holds in the smell of everything that's been in it. A big cave has enough air circulating inside it so it only gets a dank odor," he told her, dismounted, and went outside, where he lighted two long twigs, and brought them back inside. The cave was more than large enough, with an L-shaped section at the rear, and he put the twigs down inside the back section, added more wood until the fire was large enough to fill the area with warmth. Lisa dropped to her knees beside the flame, still shivering, as he returned with the blanket, which had stayed dry inside the saddlebag.

He began to strip off his wet clothes and she glanced at him, returned her eyes to the fire. "You'll never get warm with those wet clothes on," he said, and she didn't answer. "You going to take them off or do you want me to do it for you?" he said.

Her black eyes lifted, met his, and she began to undo the wet blouse. Fargo stripped away the last of his own clothes, watched as she shed the blouse, the deep, magnificently curved breasts swaying gently as she moved, pulled off her skirt and half-slip. Not

94

looking at him, she knelt beside the fire again, hands folded across the dense, jet triangle, eyes downcast, looking like a penitent, a nakedly gorgeous penitent.

He stirred the fire higher and stretched out on the blanket beside her. She stayed staring into the fire, her voice small. "You think they're looking for us by now?"

"Probably," he said. "But they won't be finding us, not even if they come up this way. The fire's back too far to show a glow outside."

She continued to stare into the flames, letting him see the side of only one beautifully rounded breast, the edge of the tiny point. "I guess that makes two I owe you," she said.

"Two?" he queried.

"The Shoshoni and getting us out just now," she said.

"Try three," he said blandly, saw her cast a quick frown at him, look away instantly. "That first afternoon in bed," he added.

This time she snapped the frown back. "You'd no choice then. You had to do that," she said.

"I didn't have to make it good for you. You owe me for that," he said.

Anger flew into the black eyes, but she didn't change her position. "No, I don't. I hate you for that," she said.

Fargo's frown was uncomprehending. "For making the best of it for you?" he questioned.

"Yes," she almost shouted. "I didn't want that. I wanted it to be horrible. I wanted it to be full of pain and disgust, an experience I'd never stop loathing. I wanted you to be rough, horrible. I hated giving myself. I wanted it to be my punishment for what I was doing. I didn't want anything to be good about it, nothing."

His eyes narrowed on her. "But you enjoyed it. I made you enjoy it," he said slowly.

The black orbs stayed on him and he saw her breasts rise as she drew in deep breaths. "Yes, damn you," she half-whispered. "All I've done is remember how good it was, think about how wonderful it could be."

"It's time you stopped thinking about it," Fargo said, reached out, pulled her around to him.

"No," she started to protest, but his hand closed around one full breast. "Oh, oh . . ." she gasped, threw her head backward, and her eyes closed. The long jet hair seemed a black waterfall as it cascaded down her back. His thumb moved slowly across the tiny nipple. "Oh, oh, oh . . . oh, my God," she breathed, and he saw her hands opening and closing against her abdomen. He pushed her down on the blanket, almost roughly, as his mouth closed around her breast, drawing gently, pulling it deeper into his mouth. The fire had done its task and her breast was sweet warmness, soft and mouth-filling, and he heard her little cries beginning, small, sharp sounds that came with each pull of his lips.

Her arms lifted, suddenly were around him, pulling tight, and he rolled with her, buried his face between her breasts. "Fargo," he heard her say. "Please, Fargo, oh, yes, please." Her legs drew up, fell wide for him, and he felt the sweet roughness of the dense, jet triangle brushing against him. She pushed upward, using her hips to say what her lips failed to say, asking, pleading with the warm wetness of other lips, and he moved, rested the tip of his throbbing maleness against the edge of the eager portal. She half-screamed, a low sound at first, quickly rising. "Yes, oh, yes . . . please, please . . . aaaah . . ." she managed to gasp out. Slowly, with excruciating pleasure, he slid forward and her hands dug into his ribs. "Aaaaaah . . . oh, oh, ooooh . . ." she breathed, and as he slipped deeper into her, the words became only sounds, soft moanings that rose and fell as he moved back and forth inside her. He began to quicken his pace and her sounds grew deeper, louder, and he felt her fingers digging deeper into his sides. He pulled one full breast into his mouth as he moved inside her, felt the tiny point now a soft hardness, and he touched his tongue to it, circled, and she lifted her head backward, her mouth parted in silent ecstasy.

The long, thick black locks fell partially over her shoulders, strayed onto the deep breasts and formed a soft veil that swayed as her breasts swayed. He was moving faster inside her now and suddenly he saw the black liquid eyes snap open. She stared up at him, half-frowning, a combination of sudden panic and pleasure forming inside the deep orbs. Her breath began to sputter in tiny gasps. "Oh, my, oh, my . . . it . . . it . . . it's happening. . . . Oh, oh . . . oh, my." He saw her swallow, her lips come open, and she was trying to form words but no sound came, and then he felt her closing around him, a sudden contraction. He laughed with his own surge of pleasure, thrust forward, and watched her black eyes, which seemed to stare in disbelief, unable to completely accept the rush of ecstasy that was shooting through her body. Her lips opened wider, stayed that way as the scream came from her, bursting forth, an outer explosion to match the inner one. Her pelvis thrust hard against him as he pushed into the deepest recess of her throbbing cavity and her legs slammed hard against his sides, pressed, quivered against him. The scream hung in the air and her eyes remained open, wide, black depths of unbelief.

Slowly the stark fervency in the swimming deep of her eyes began to lessen and her legs fell away from him as he felt her abdomen quiver. She gulped in deep drafts of air and the scream became a low sound of awesome wonderment. He moved gently inside her, finally drawing back. "Aaaaaah . . . oh, my God . . . aaaah," she moaned as he pulled from the warm enveloping of her. She stretched her body, legs drawing out straight, and her hands moved over the thick muscles of his chest and the liquid black eyes continued to stare up at him.

"It's always better the second time," Fargo said, smiled at her, and her eyes searched his face as she nodded, studied him for a long moment.

"Why did you make that first time good, everything that I didn't want it to be?" she asked. "Kindness? A soft spot in you?"

"No, couldn't help it," he said blandly, and she frowned the question at him. He shrugged. "A good horseman can't give a bad ride," he said.

Her eyes narrowed a fraction at him and she lay back, the full breasts pointing upward at him.

"No more modesty?" he said.

She half-shrugged. "Doesn't seem right anymore," she said, lay invitingly before him. He took in the spectacular beauty of her, the firelight tinting her breasts a soft orange, her abdomen a tiny convexity, and her hips full and magnificently curved. Every inch of her was molded, shaped, fashioned with beauty. "I never knew, never dreamed it could be so—so overwhelming," she said, groping for words.

"Your beauty is made for it," he said. "You're made to feel, enjoy, want, and be wanted, the way a flower is meant to blossom and be beautiful."

She looked away and her face grew clouded. "It's all turned out so differently, not the way I'd planned at all. I wish I had it to do over again. I wish I could wipe out everything that's happened," she said.

He let his fingers circle the tiny nipple of one breast. "Everything?" he echoed.

Her face turned back to his and a tiny smile came to edge her lips. "All right, not everything," she said, slid arms up to encircle his neck, pulled his head down to her breasts. "Make the flower blossom again," she breathed, and he felt her belly press upward against him. She turned to place one sweet warm breast against his lips, gasped softly as he took it into his mouth. One taste of honey was never enough, he murmured inwardly as he settled down to enjoy her newfound wanting. It was nearly dawn when the cave stopped echoing the gasped murmurs of ecstasy and she slept hard against him.

6

He was dressed and standing at the mouth of the cave when she woke and appeared still buttoning the lemon blouse. His eyes traveled up and down the land as she halted at his side. "See anything?" she asked.

"No," he answered, still scanning the sunlit morning foliage. "Didn't expect to. They're back at Bart Bullmer's by now, trying to explain how they had us and lost us."

"Which way do we run now? Straight south?" Lisa asked.

"No running anywhere," Fargo said, turning to her to see the disbelief form in her black eyes.

"You can't mean that," she said. "I don't believe you."

"Try harder," he said.

"Then last night didn't mean anything to you," she said, sounded hurt.

"It was great, but it didn't take my neck off the line," he said.

"I thought after last night you'd want to get away, just run with me," she said.

"I'm too polite," he said.

"Polite?" She frowned.

"I hate to screw and run." He smiled affably as

she spun on her heel and stalked away. She was beside the gelding when he returned to the back of the cave, glared at him as he appeared.

"Bullmer won't listen, damn you," she flung at him.

"You said we couldn't get away last night. Saddle up," he answered, began to carry his saddle to the pinto. She followed his orders in silent anger, stayed that way as he led her out of the cave and into the foothills once again. He turned the pinto north, focused on three hills in the hazy distance. "Up there?" he asked, and Lisa nodded, her lips tight. Fargo estimated time and distance. By midday by ordinary riding, by dusk the way they'd move, stopping to scan every rise and valley, staying inside timberlines, using extra care and caution at every turn. He guided the pinto forward as Lisa continued to shower angry silence over him.

A little past noon he halted in the deep cool of a tanbark oak glen where the thick grass was soft as a carpet. He rested the horses, let them nibble the rich grass, and watched Lisa sit down, her distance a silent comment. He smiled as he walked to her, stood before her, and she glared up at him.

"You never know," he commented idly.

"You never know what?" she snapped.

"When it'll be the last chance," he said. "I don't like wasting last chances."

Her eyes stayed glowering, watched as he unbuttoned his trousers, focused on the growing bulge inside the cloth. Her tongue flicked across her lips. He let the bulge push itself out of the opening and she drew a sharp breath in as her lips parted. "Damn you, Fargo," she breathed. "Oh, damn you."

He took one step to her and the little gasped cry came from her as she fell forward, hands grasping for him, clutching, caressing. She clung to his organ as she fell backward, lifting her hips, tearing the skirt down from her, and in moments the little glen grew warm with the heat of wanting, two forms intertwined, the little cries of pleasure echoing softly in the silence. This time the disbelief in the overwhelming ecstasy no longer filled the deep eyes. This time he saw the dark hunger of wanting, almost a devouring, a deep, dark fire as she cried out with his every thrust. "Oh, my God, oh, Fargo . . . oh, yes, oh, yes, yes, yes . . ." she murmured, words falling into each other, sweet mumblings, and he felt her come into rhythm with his every movement and her pleasure became still another wonderful discovery. "Yes, oh, my God, oh, how wonderful . . . wonderful . . . oh, God, yes," she continued to gasp out, a chant of ecstasy.

He buried his face into Lisa's magnificent breasts, reveled in the soft touch of their smoothness, began to push into her with long thrusts that reached to the deepest part of her, and he felt her legs rise, clasp around his buttocks. Little crying calls came from her, a gasped chorus to match his every deep thrust, and then her hips lifted, her hands digging into the back of his neck, pressing his face against her breasts. Her pelvis moved convulsively and there was only a long wordless cry from her parted lips, and he felt the warm envelope growing warmer, contracting, expanding, quivering around him in a silent explosion of passion. He stayed in her until she fell back, breathing hard, the black eyes open wide to stare at him, once again touched with wonder, the inability to embrace the overwhelming power of her own ecstasy.

"Too much," she breathed. "Too much."

"And not enough," he said.

She nodded slowly. "And not enough," she agreed.

He lay beside her, let his body cool, finally rose and pulled on trousers. She lifted herself up at once and stood before him. "Stay with me, Fargo," she said.

He half-smiled. "You mean run with you," he returned.

Her tiny half-shrug was one of admission. "I'd be yours, Fargo, for always. Anywhere you wanted to go," she said. She stood proudly before him, suddenly all temptress, using the power of beauty, the strength of sex.

He didn't hide the ruefulness in his smile. "It'd be nice," he admitted. "But I've still got promises to keep. I've got to keep traveling alone."

"Promises can wait, for a little while, anyway," she said, pleading coloring her tone.

"Not mine," he said, his voice growing hard at once. "Get your clothes on," he ordered.

He started to turn from her, but she caught at his arm, pulled him back. "Why? Have I too much of an advantage this way?" she slid at him, suddenly full of smugness and guile.

He half-laughed. "Almost," he said. "But only almost."

Her arms came around his neck and she pressed the full, deeply curved breasts against his chest, a soft, warm pressure. "Those promises, they must be very special," she remarked.

"Because you can't turn me away from them?" he answered.

"Maybe," she conceded, half-pouted.

"Don't feel bad. There've been plenty others who tried and failed," he said.

"Then they must be very special promises," she said, and the guile and pout left her and he saw only searching honesty in the deep black orbs. "Tell me about them, Fargo," she asked.

"Not a lot to tell. I had a family once. Three dirty, stinkin' gunslingers wiped them out, my pa, my ma, and my brother," he said. "One of them's paid for it. There are two more to go."

"You going to spend your whole life chasing them?" she asked.

"I don't expect it'll take that long," he said. "But their accounts are called in now. They just don't know it yet."

"I'd wait for you," she said softly.

"You're not made for waiting," he said. "Get dressed. One thing at a time."

He turned, started back to get the horses, heard her hiss of anger follow him. "Dammit, you can't keep those promises if you're a dead man," she called out. He half-smiled as he kept walking. She could change directions like a polo pony. Fear or instinct? he wondered. Maybe a little of each.

She was dressed when he brought the horses back and she swung onto the gelding with her lips set tight. Fargo set a course hugging the edge of tree clusters, moving into the open only when there was no other choice. The day was drawing to a close when he halted at the edge of a stand of cottonwoods, gestured to a steep pathway to the right. "We'll go up that way," he said.

"Why?" Lisa questioned. "We could go straight here."

"There are three riders on top of the ridgeline in front of us, four more on this level over in those aspens," Fargo said calmly.

Lisa frowned as she peered out beyond the treeline. "I don't see anything at all," she muttered.

"That's because you're looking to see people," he told her. "You look for movement first, then you find what causes it." He started up the steep pathway, waved at her to follow. "They're there, believe me," he said.

The path grew steeper and he slowed as the big footed gelding had trouble pulling upward, but they reached the top and he let the horses rest for a moment. Only one hill remained, lower than the others, and he started for it, his eyes scanning every foot of the land. He halted suddenly as they started down the last of the slopes. He sat very still in the saddle, his face turned upward into the wind.

"We're close," he said.

"How do you know?" Lisa frowned.

"Cut logs, they have their own smell. So do clothes hung on a line to dry," Fargo said.

She studied his high-cheekboned, intense handsomeness. "I wonder if you're more animal than human. Maybe that's why they say you're the best, the Trailsman," she reflected.

"Smelling and hearing, they're as important as seeing if you want to stay alive in the wild country," he said.

She gave a little snort. "You don't want to stay alive. You want to commit suicide and you're taking me with you," she tossed at him.

"You started it all, honey, and you're going to finish it with me," he returned, sent the pinto forward. The slope ended, became a rise of black oak, and he threaded his way through the trees until he reached the end of the rise, a high place that let him look down in the rapidly fading light of dusk. The logging camp lay spread out beneath him, built on the sloping side of a hill. A river ran below the camp at the bottom of the slope and he let his eyes travel across the camp, a fast glance at first, then a slow, careful scrutiny. It was a place of sheds and lean-tos with two more substantial bunkhouses across from each other. The main house stood alone, not much more than a larger version of the bunkhouses. A long line of cut timber ran up one side of the hill, contained in a long chute and held in place by a wooden gate at the bottom. The chute was positioned so that, when it was opened, the logs would roll down the slope and into the river at the bottom.

Logging camps were never much on looks, but this one was shoddier and dirtier than most, Fargo noted. It sprawled with mounds of uncut branches and piles of garbage left lying about. His eyes passed over the three wash lines of shirts and Levi's hung from two trees. A half-dozen men struggled with a long log, using ropes and chains to pull it into the chute with the other logs. As Fargo watched, his eyes narrowed; he saw seven riders return to the camp and put their horses into what was obviously a crude barn to one side of camp. He was scanning the perimeters, figuring out the best entry and exit points, when Lisa pulled on his sleeve. "Bart Bullmer," she whispered.

He followed her gaze to the figure that had stepped from the main house, and he wondered how the man had got himself through the door. Bart Bullmer weighed close to three hundred pounds, he guessed, with a face that seemed to fold over itself in great hanging globs of flesh. Tiny pig eyes were almost lost in that face of thick lips and heavy jowls, an overbearing, bloated face topped by a completely bald head that grew out of a series of fat layers that served as a neck. But the gross figure was not all fat, Fargo took note. Under the massive expanse of flesh there was not only weight but muscle, as Bart Bullmer's short-sleeved shirt revealed arms the thickness of small trees.

The men emerged from the barn and two reported to Bullmer, and Fargo frowned as he saw the man's tiny pig eyes lift, sweep the slopes that surrounded his logging camp, slowly return to the two men. Lisa's question echoed the thought that suddenly stabbed at him.

"What's that mean, his looking around that way?" she asked.

"I don't know. Probably nothing," Fargo said.

"You think those riders saw us?" she pressed.

"No," he said. He was certain of that, but he didn't tell her they might have come upon their tracks. It was an outside chance and he pushed it aside, swung down from the saddle. "We wait now," he said tethering the horse.

"For what?" she asked as she dismounted.

"For Big Bart to hit the sack," Fargo said, sat down against a tree that gave him a full view of the logging camp. Lisa settled herself, her beautiful features drawn tight with anger.

"Suicide. Madness," she grumbled.

Fargo ignored her mutterings, watched the camp settle down as night blanketed the land. Light from inside the buildings stayed on until supper was over and let him see figures moving back and forth across the camp and between the bunkhouses. At one point he saw the door of the main house open and Bart Bullmer's huge form sidled outside, light from the open door at his back outlining the great bulk of the man. As Fargo watched, a figure came out of the darkness and paused before Bullmer, the man with the bandanna Lisa had called a convicted horse thief. When he finally walked away into the darkness, Bart Bullmer edged his girth through the door again, closed it behind him.

The camp grew silent soon after, but Fargo let time pass and the night grow long.

"What are you waiting for?" Lisa hissed finally. "They've all been asleep long ago."

Fargo pointed to the moon that had finally risen

high enough to outline the buildings in its pale silver light. He rose onto one knee, his eyes slowly traveling the edges of the camp, shifting down to the area around the main house. He made a second careful sweep with his eyes and felt less uneasy. "No guards posted," he said. "Nobody said anything to make him expect trouble." He rose, gestured to Lisa. "Let's go," he said.

"You go," she answered. "You've a better chance to get through alone." Fargo eyed her. "Bring him back here," Lisa said.

Her words were true enough. He would stand a better chance alone. He almost smiled. "And you'll be waiting right here, of course. You're not seeing a perfect chance to hightail it, are you?"

She managed to summon indignation. "Aren't you ever going to trust me?" she asked.

He half-shrugged. "Maybe. Another time, another place," he said, his voice flat. "Let's go." He watched her lips tighten onto each other as she threw a glare at him, pulled herself to her feet. "You stay right behind me. You step exactly where I step, understand?" Fargo said, and she nodded. He turned, began to start down the slope, moving out of the trees. He moved slowly and carefully, deliberately, to let Lisa follow his every step. He avoided twigs on the ground, loose stones, and dry brush, made his way down the slope until he reached the long chute of logs. Creeping alongside it, he stayed in the deepest shadows until he halted across from the main house and sank down on one knee. He felt Lisa against his back.

"Only one doorway in," he muttered, surveyed the area near the house. Nothing moved, no shadowed figures waited. He started toward the corner of the house, Lisa close at his heels, and he glanced at her. There was fear stark in the black round eyes. He halted at the door of the house, closed one big hand around the doorknob, and inched the knob around until he felt it release with an almost noiseless click. He eased the door open and slipped into the house as Lisa followed. A night lamp burned low to one side of a crudely furnished room, wood chairs and a bearskin rug making up most of the furnishings. A door to another room hung open near the dim lamp and the unmistakable sound of heavy snoring came from inside the room. Fargo moved soundlessly toward the room, winced at Lisa's footsteps behind him. He halted at the doorway, the lamplight flickering into the room. His glance passed over the two windows, each half open, to the lone four-poster bed that occupied the room.

The huge form of Bart Bullmer seemed even more mountainous asleep, making the big bed look too small. He wore a dirty gray undershirt and torn long johns, Fargo saw as he stepped into the room. But the big man was a light sleeper and Fargo saw the tiny pig's eyes snap open. The big Colt was in his hand instantly, pressing into the folds of Bart Bullmer's face. Fargo pushed the end of the barrel deeper into the fat jowls and the tiny eyes blinked. They flicked to Lisa, back to the tall black-haired man in front of him.

"You're him, the one on the Ovaro," Bullmer growled. "The one they call the Trailsman."

Fargo nodded, stepped back a pace as Bullmer slid down from the bed, moving the huge bulk with surprising ease.

"You must be crazy coming here," Bullmer said.

"Just tired of you trying to have me killed," Fargo said.

"I got reason," the man said. "And you're as good as dead now."

"You've got no reason. You've been making a mistake," Fargo said. "That's why I'm here. The little lady has something to tell you."

Bart Bullmer's little eyes went to Lisa, contempt in them, and Fargo saw her half-turn, stare at him. She seemed frozen, her throat swallowing rapidly.

"Start talking," Fargo said to her, and she stared past him. Slowly she brought her glance back to Bullmer. "Talk," Fargo hissed at her.

Lisa's eyes stayed on Bullmer. "If I tell you the truth, you'll let me go?" she asked.

"I got no use for you," the man said, his voice a low rumble.

"You'll let me go, your word on it?" Lisa asked.

Bullmer shrugged. "Anytime. I don't want you now," he growled.

"Tell him, dammit," Fargo rasped.

Lisa's eyes, round with fear, stayed on Big Bart, and she licked the dryness of her lips with a flick of her tongue. "Fargo brought me here to tell you that it wasn't his fault, none of it. He wants me to tell you that he was forced into taking me and that I planned it all so you wouldn't have me," she said, paused, flicked a glance at Fargo, then brought her eyes back to Bullmer. "But it's all a lie. I didn't force him to do anything. He saw me riding and he just grabbed me and took me," she blurted out.

Fargo felt the surprise flood his face as he whirled at her. "You lying little bitch," he half-roared.

Lisa's eyes stayed riveted on Bart Bullmer. "He made me come here. He said he'd kill me if I didn't say what he wanted me to say," she went on.

"*Goddamn!*" Fargo swore, spun the Colt back as he saw Bullmer start toward him out of the corner of his eye. "Don't move," Fargo warned, the Colt aimed straight at the man's chest.

"You too, mister," he heard the voice say. It came from the open window to his right and he half-turned his head, saw the three rifle muzzles poked over the windowsill, all aimed dead at him.

"Over here, too," he heard another voice say, this one from the other half-open window. He didn't bother to turn, let a deep breath out as he lowered the Colt. Bart Bullmer's huge arm reached out and took the gun from his hand. Fargo's mouth was a thin line as the grim realization swept through him. The off chance he'd pushed aside had become a reality. He'd been expected. His eyes met Bart Bullmer's glittering little orbs.

"Your boys came onto our tracks," he muttered.

"That's right. But I couldn't be sure then. I told the boys to stay out of sight inside the bunkhouse and just keep their eyes on that front door of mine," Bart Bullmer said as Fargo watched the others clamber in through the windows, rifles still held on him. Lisa's voice cut through his silent curses.

"Can I get out of here now?" she asked Bullmer.

The folds of the gross face moved aside enough for a thick-lipped smile to emerge. "I don't want you. You're used goods and you know I don't touch used goods," the man said. "But my boys don't feel the same way."

"You promised," Lisa began, and Bullmer cut her off.

"Shut up," he barked. "I only said I'd let you go." He gestured to two of the men. "Get her out of here," he said, and the men started to pull Lisa away. "But only one night, you hear me. I don't want no trash around my camp for more than one night, understand?" he ordered.

The men nodded. Lisa's glance met Fargo's eyes for an instant and his rage exploded. "Lying little bitch, you deserve whatever you get," he flung at her.

She disappeared out the door, the men holding her

arms, and Fargo saw Bullmer turn his huge bulk toward him. "Now, you're as good as dead, but not right away. I wanted that little thing. Oh, my, how I wanted her, had my eye on her for the past three years. And you went and ruined her for me, took away somethin' I really wanted. You're going to pay for that, mister. You're going to pay."

One of the treelike arms shot out, a huge fist at the end of it. Fargo tightened his stomach muscles, but the blow still felt as though a mule had kicked him in the stomach. He sailed backward, crashed into the wall, and dropped to the floor, drew his knees up as the pain in his stomach almost made him sick.

"Take him into the big room and string him up. You know what to do," he heard Bullmer order, felt hands lift him, half-drag him out into the other room. The lamp was turned up and he regained some of his breath, tried to shake off the grip on his arms, and received a blow from behind that made his head spin. Dimly he felt clothes being pulled from him and he shook his head, fought consciousness back as his arms were raised. He felt the ropes tying his wrists together, then onto a cross beam. He shook his head, finally cleared it, and saw he was hanging naked from the cross beam, his feet touching the floor. He saw Bart Bullmer, his tiny pig eyes glittering with cruelty and anticipated pleasure, move around him, examine his muscled body.

"Strong bastard, isn't he?" the man muttered. "That's real good. He won't be passing out too quickly." Bullmer halted in front of him and Fargo met the little eyes, which now glistened with excitement. "But not for a few hours, not till dawn. I need my sleep," the man said.

Fargo saw him wave an arm and the other three men left, closed the door behind them. Bullmer stepped up to him again, drew his arm back, and smashed a blow into Fargo's belly, and the Trailsman felt himself sway backward, his knees sagging, but the ropes holding him kept him dangling. Bart Bullmer laughed, a harsh, rumbling sound as he strode away and disappeared into the other room.

Fargo tightened shoulder and arm muscles, tested the ropes that held him suspended from the beam. He tried twisting his wrists, pulled downward with all his strength, ended up cursing under his breath. The ropes hadn't the slightest hint of give in them and he decided not to waste his strength further. He'd need every ounce of it come dawn, he was certain. Bart Bullmer was plainly a man who enjoyed cruelty, the tiny pig eyes the eyes of a backwoods sadist. There'd be nothing refined in Bullmer's methods. Only sheer pain.

The window behind him was open and he could hear the shouts and laughter coming from the bunkhouse, interspersed with Lisa's screams and he listened to the screams as they changed in character, going from fear to anger to pain and back again. They were roughing her up as much as enjoying her. Good, he spit out silently. She'd been a lying little bitch. He'd thought he had reached her, but she'd shown him differently. Once again she proved that she cared only about her own self, her actions those of an unprincipled, amoral little viper hiding behind a mask of consummate beauty. He'd allow himself no sympathy for her, and he closed his ears until the night grew silent and the men in the bunkhouse tired of their fun.

He let his muscles hang, tried to relax the tensions inside them. The night wore on slowly as his shoulders began to ache until he became conscious of the gray light of dawn slipping, almost as if reluctant, into the room. With it, the huge form of Bart Bullmer appeared in the doorway, clad in trousers and still wearing the gray undershirt, folds of fat hanging over the muscles of his sloping shoulders. Fargo straightened, watched the man approach, and his eyes fastened on the bullwhip in Big Bart's hand.

The man raised the whip, a short-handled version, snapped it in the air, and his eyes were tiny circles of hard brightness. "This'll be just for starters, big boy," Bullmer growled. He stepped back and sent the whip whistling through the air. Fargo braced himself as the whip slashed across his naked body, a diagonal slash across his chest, and he grimaced at the sharp pain. Bullmer circled, snapped the whip again, and this time it came from the side to slash across Fargo's ribs. The huge figure circled again, and as Fargo felt the whip cut into his buttocks, a gasp of pain escaped his lips. Bullmer began to circle faster, the whip lashing out with greater speed, coming in from all sides. The pain grew intense, searing, and Fargo felt his skin tearing, long red welts rising across his entire body. Bullmer was laughing, a roaring, gurgled sound, as he slashed the whip across every part of Fargo's naked body, arms, chest, back, thighs, midsection.

He paused for a moment and Fargo fought through the pain that throbbed through his entire frame to see Bart Bullmer perspiring heavily, his tiny pig eyes glistening with sadistic glee. In horror, he saw Bullmer bend low, send the whip whistling through the air, his aim accurate, and Fargo felt the slashing thong curl around his testicles. His roar of pain mingled with Bullmer's bellowing laughter, and he felt himself go limp as waves of pain drew away what remaining strength he had. His body sagged and he hung swaying from the beam, the pain in his groin a burning, sucking fire. He heard the door open and Bullmer's voice rumbling orders.

"Take him down and put him in the shed," he heard the man say. Hands grabbed at him, pulled, lifted, and his arms fell to his sides as the wrist ropes were undone. Somehow, he kept his feet, drew on an inner strength, and they led him to a small shed behind the house. He fell as they flung him inside and his torn, bleeding skin scraped along the floor as he heard the door slam shut, a bolt go into place. He lay still, his body on fire, crisscrossed with long red welts and strips of bleeding, torn skin. His arm muscles seemed flaccid, stretched from the hours of hanging suspended. The cool wood of the floor was a welcome touch to his naked body and he put his head down, lay half-curled, his knees drawn up. Hours dragged on before the searing pain began to subside and he lay unmoving, half-asleep, half-awake, finally lapsing into a full sleep.

When he woke, he pushed himself up to a sitting position, blinked his eyes clear. The little shed was dim, but he could hear the sounds of men at work outside, shouts and curses, chains pulling logs, the snorting of workhorses. The cracks in the wood of the shed were not wide enough to see out, but they let a little air and daylight seep into the shed. It was a windowless place, he saw, and he slowly, painfully, pulled himself to his feet, cried out in pain. His skin seemed to crack as he stretched, and he forced himself to fight down the sharp, burning pain. The long red welts covered his body, he saw, and he stretched again. His muscle tone had returned and he was grateful for that. Bullmer wasn't finished with him, and he steeled himself for what was still in store for him. He wondered if they'd finally thrown Lisa out. Probably, he decided, remembering Bullmer's orders. The men weren't likely to cross Bart Bullmer.

Fargo lay down again, stretched his back over the coolness of the wood floor, letting the touch soothe the rawness of his body. He slept again after a while, finally woke to find the shed pitch black. Night had come. He rose, went to the door, and put his shoulder against it. He exerted a slow, steady pressure. There was give in the wood but not enough, and the bolt held securely. He swore, stepped back, his mind racing. There was a chance. Surprise was always a weapon. He lay down on the floor again, drew his knees up, lay facedown. He was that way when he heard the voices outside, listened to the bolt being pushed back. The door came open, a swirl of night breeze sweeping over him. He didn't move.

"Get up," he heard a voice call out. He remained motionless.

"Move," another voice said. There were at least two of them, he noted, continued to remain motionless. He heard footsteps coming toward him. A figure reached down, grabbed his arm, started to pull him around. Fargo's leg shot out, caught the man in the groin.

"*Agh!*" the figure gasped as it doubled over. Fargo rolled, coming up on his knees, dived for the second figure as the man started to raise a rifle. He barreled into the second figure, carried the man half out the door with him when he glimpsed another man leaping forward, rifle butt upraised. He tried to spin away, but the rifle stock came down, a glancing blow on his head but enough to send him sprawling on his back, vision suddenly a jumbled collection of blurred shapes. He shook his head, cleared it, saw the two men standing above him. One pushed the

116

rifle barrel into his abdomen. "Son of a bitch," the man cursed.

The third man came up, one hand still holding his groin. "Kill the bastard," he breathed.

Another voice cut in sharply, the man with the bandanna. "No, you damn fool. You kill him and Bart'll cut your balls off. He ain't finished with this bastard yet," the man said. The third figure, who was still holding his groin, stepped back sullenly, let a kick fly that dug into Fargo's ribs and made him gasp out in pain. The other two pulled him to his feet, flung his naked form ahead of them, rifles pressed into the small of his back. They marched him into the house where Bullmer waited.

"Bastard tried to make a break for it," the man in the bandanna grunted.

The pig eyes glinted. "Good. Very good. That means he's still strong," Bullmer rumbled. "Tie him up, hands and feet this time." The men produced rope and Fargo's hands were tied behind his back, his ankles bound together. The men flung him to the floor and left the room. Fargo half-turned onto his back, was able to wriggle to a sitting position as he saw Bullmer take a four-foot-long piece of flat wood from a corner of the room. Fargo's eyes widened as he saw that the one side of the wood plank was studded with strips of barbed wire. Bullmer advanced on him, his little eyes glittering.

"No wonder that girl killed herself," Fargo said. "You're a goddamn pervert, Bullmer."

The man's folds of fat shook in instant anger. "You've the nerve to call me names?" he thundered.

"Why not? It's all I can do, you fat-faced fucking pervert," Fargo spit at him.

Bullmer let out a roar of rage, raised his arm, and Fargo buried his face into the floor as the board came down across his back. His scream was muffled by the floorboards as his back seemed to explode in pain. Bullmer grasped at his arm, pulled him around, started to bring the board down again. Fargo kicked out with both bound-together feet, aimed at the expanse of groin in front of him. But Bullmer, for all his bulk, was quick enough to bring the board down, and Fargo's feet struck into it with full force.

"Ow, Jesus," Fargo screamed as he drew back, saw the splatter of blood fly through the air from the bottoms of his feet. He half-turned again as Bullmer came down with the board. This time the blow hit him across the buttocks, the barbed wire twisting into his flesh. Again and again the board came down as Fargo rolled and wriggled across the floor, trying to escape the shower of pain. But it was a useless task and soon he lay still, bleeding from a hundred cuts and tears, his body on fire, the pain consuming, obliterating. He lay with his cheek against the floor, his breath drawn out in rasping gasps, and he wished he were unconscious. For the first time in his life, he cursed the strength that was his.

He heard Bart Bullmer's heavy breathing, felt the man yank his head back by the hair, and he stared up at the bald-headed, gross face as Bullmer bent low to him. "Can you hear me, bastard?" the man asked, holding his head pulled back. Fargo nodded as the pain continued to envelop him. "I want you to be able to think about tomorrow night," Bullmer rumbled. "I'm going to hang you up by your prick, you hear me. Then I'm going to watch until it tears off. You won't be putting it in anything that belongs to me again."

He let go of Fargo's hair and Fargo felt himself being pulled by the legs; he wanted to scream in pain as his torn and bleeding body was dragged across the floor, but he'd no more voice left. Bullmer dragged him to the little shack, opened the door, and flung him inside.

As Fargo lay there, he brought the barbed-wire board down on his back and buttocks again, boomed out a roar of satisfaction. Fargo dimly heard the bolt sliding into place on the door and then he felt the grayness slipping over him. He couldn't move, his entire body consumed in pain, this time his muscles part of the flame that seemed to devour him. He welcomed the unconsciousness that came over him. Relief. Peace. Pain shut away. He lay there, an inert, unconscious form, blood seeping from a hundred holes and tears in his body.

The night had grown deep when his eyelids flickered, consciousness returning in little bits and pieces, as if unwilling to disturb him. And with it the pain came back at once, growing as he became more conscious until, fully awake, he felt the waves of pain sweep over him once again. He lay unmoving, only his eyelids blinking against the floor. A thought came, stabbed at him almost maliciously. Perhaps he should have listened to Lisa. Perhaps he should have run. A bullet was quicker and cleaner than this. The thought vanished and he lay absolutely still, unwilling to add pain on pain.

His eyes closed and he hovered at the edge of unconsciousness again, a gray borderline that only made the searing pain a fraction more bearable. The half-world remained, for how long he didn't know, and suddenly fell away. His ears, sensitive despite the pain that surrounded him, caught the faint sound, the bolt being slid back. Was it tomorrow night already? he wondered. Had he lain unconscious through the day? It was all too possible. Time

119

was only for the conscious. The terrible helpless rage coursed through him. Not so soon, he heard himself mutter silently. He wasn't ready. He'd hoped for more time, enough to gather strength somehow for a last, desperate gesture. He heard the door open, footsteps enter. The last desperate gesture was to be denied him.

A figure knelt down beside him and he opened his eyes, fought down the pain as he turned his head to look up. He saw the thick jet hair streaming down. He was in a dream. Or perhaps gone beyond that. But a hand touched him—unmistakable, touch, feeling, things beyond dreams. He stared up at her and his lips tried to form the word. "Why?" he mouthed silently. His hand reached out, touched the long black hair. It was no dream. Disbelief flooded through him, fought through pain. He tried to utter another word, but she put her finger to his lips as she untied wrist and ankle ropes. He watched her get up, reach down, take his hand, and pull him to his feet. The pain of it was a burst of agony and he slipped to his knees, his arms clasped around her legs. "Wait," he managed to breathe, and she stayed against him.

He tried again and she helped pull him up. Once again his body seemed on fire, but he stayed on his feet, tried a step, and almost cried out as the torn, bleeding bottoms of his feet screamed in protest.

"Walk, you've got to walk," she whispered, and he nodded, took another step, and forced the groan of pain to stay inside him. Lisa's arm around his waist helped support him and he reached the ground, almost fell again. She led him back around the edge of the house, one step at a time, each one an agonizing exercise in sheer pain. He felt his strength, what was left of it, ebbing away.

"Never . . . never make it," he whispered.

"You can. I brought the horses down lower. They're in those trees just ahead," Lisa said. Words designed to spur hope. He seized on them, forced himself on, fell to his knees twice, struggled up again. He reached the trees, but his eyes were blurred and he just managed to make out the outline of the pinto. Lisa led him to the side of the horse and he fell against the warm fur, held himself up by gripping the saddle horn.

"Can't ride," he muttered. "Can't sit the saddle. Never."

"Lay across it," Lisa said. She got her shoulders under him, pushed and lifted, and this time he did cry out in pain as his body fell across the saddle, head down over the other side of the pinto. But the saddle was smooth to his torn skin, smooth and cool. The flood of relief was too much after the ordeal, his strength gone. He felt himself slip into unconsciousness again, grateful once more for the peace it brought.

He lay draped across the saddle, unconscious, aware of neither time, nor place, nor existence. When he finally came around, it was a half-waking, the touch of warmth on his back, and his eyes managed to detect light, warm light. Slowly, as though his mind were sleepwalking, he gathered in the thought. Sunlight. He felt sunlight on his back. The single thought seemed a terrible effort, and it trailed away, slipped into the gray of nothingness again as his eyes closed.

A red fox lifted its head from a blueberry patch, sharp eyes alert to the sound of intruders. It saw the horses slowly moving up the hills, a girl on a brown gelding, thick black hair streaming back from her face. She lead a striking Ovaro with a naked man draped across the saddle, his body swaying gently

121

with the movement of the horse. The red fox watched the strange procession go on deeper into the hills and put his head back into the blueberry patch.

7

His eyes came open with effort. He saw only grayness, first. He blinked once, twice, and the grayness lifted. It was replaced by blackness as he stared upward into a dark void. No, the darkness flickered, little waves of light dancing through it, and he strained his eyes into focus, saw a curved rock ceiling above him. He began to feel the pain again, but no longer overwhelming, a dull throb instead of a consuming fire. He let his eyes follow the stone ceiling downward, saw it become a wall of rock. He lay inside a cave, the realization coming slowly to him.

He pushed himself up on one elbow and felt the pain spiral up throughout his body, instantly intense. He fought it down, stayed on one elbow, and let his eyes follow the wall of the cave, saw a fire burning a few feet from him, and beyond that an L-shaped section. He frowned, slow recognition moving through him. The cave was familiar and he tried to hold on to the thought. It took effort. Everything took effort and the pain was growing intense again. He dropped back, drew in deep breaths as he stared at the rock ceiling.

He tried to focus his thoughts, reach back. It had all been so dim, everything seen out of a haze of semiconsciousness. The pain subsided some when he lay back, but he felt something on his body. He had been naked, he remembered that with a flash of clarity, and he bent his head forward to see that he was covered with leaves and cloths. He heard footsteps, lifted his head again despite the pain, and saw Lisa appear. She carried a load of wood in her arms, her eyes finding him at once. She put the wood down, fell to her knees beside him, the liquid black eyes peering at him with apprehension and concern.

"You're awake," she said, her hand touching his forehead. "Your eyes are clear," she said, satisfaction touching her lips.

He swallowed, licked his lips, found a voice that didn't even sound like his own, a hoarse, weak rasp. "How long. . . ?" he tried, and she cut him off.

"Don't try to talk. You need to rest more," she said.

"No," he managed to protest. "Tell me. How long have we been here?"

"Since this morning. I remembered the way back," she said.

"I've been out all that time?" he asked.

"You half-woke three or four times, but slipped off again almost instantly. It was the best thing for you," Lisa told him.

"I don't hurt as much. I'm not on fire," he said.

"Sage leaves and poultices of Solomon's seal and mugwort juice. My ma taught me about them, best thing for cuts and sores," Lisa said.

Fargo started to push up on one elbow, gasped at the wave of pain that shot through his body, and Lisa pushed him back down. "No, you've got a lot of healing to do yet. You're hurt real bad and you lost a lot of blood. You look like a human sieve," she said.

Fargo looked up at her as she leaned half over

124

him. She had a bruised cheekbone, another welt across her temple. And she still looked beautiful. Memory pulled at him. Nothing fitted, nothing explained itself. "Tell me, Lisa," he said. "Make sense out of it for me. Start from the beginning."

"Why I lied to Bart Bullmer?" she said.

"Yes." He nodded. "Why didn't you just tell him the truth then?"

"I saw his boys at the window with their rifles. I couldn't say anything to you. They'd have killed you if you'd turned," she said. "I knew if I told Big Bart the truth he'd just have us both killed. I put it all on you once again," she said, paused, met his waiting eyes. "I knew one of us had to get away and I had the best chance. He didn't want me anymore. He just wanted his revenge."

"But he tossed you to his boys," Fargo said.

Her lips turned in a rueful half-smile. "It didn't work out exactly as I'd planned, but it worked," she said.

Fargo lingered on the bruises, remembered her screams. "It was bad, wasn't it?" he said.

"It could've been worse," she said. "They roughed me up first, especially Ezzner, the one with the bandanna. But they got drunk and started fighting over me. By the time they were finished, they were too drunk and too beat to bother me much anymore. I expected they'd really have at me the next night, but Bullmer was real mad at them in the morning. He made them toss me out."

"Where'd you go?" Fargo asked.

"I ran, let them think I was going to keep running forever," she said.

"You could have," he half-whispered.

Her eyes held his. "I could have, and never be able to look in a mirror again," she said.

Fargo reached a hand to her, winced in pain. "I

125

owe you. I had you figured all wrong," he said. His hand fell away and he felt weak.

"I'm the one owing," Lisa said. "For all of it, from the very beginning." Her hand stroked his forehead. "No more talk now. You just lie still. I'm going to change your poultices for fresh ones."

She rose, left for a moment, knelt by the fire, and then he felt her removing the leaves and the cloths from his entire body. She was so gentle he hardly felt her hands upon him. "A sieve, a damn sieve, that's what he's made out of you," he heard her murmur as she began to apply fresh leaves and fresh cloths soaked in her concoction. He felt the coolness drawing fire from his wounds, soothing, peaceful, the balm of gilead. He felt himself going to sleep and was unable to do anything about it.

The fresh air of morning infiltrated the cave when he woke. Lisa, looking crisply lovely in a white shirt, combed her hair nearby, and she stopped when she saw him wake, came to him at once. "I've some chamomile tea and cooked Jerusalem artichokes I dug up," she said. "You have to eat something."

As he pulled himself up on his elbows, she brought the cooked tubers, fed him with a spoon from his saddlebag. After he'd eaten, he sipped the tea from one of the tin cups in his things and then she helped him lie back on the blanket. He watched her take a warm cloth and begin to remove the leaves and other cloths. Gently she pressed the warm cloth on his skin, moving from spot to spot, cleansing the lacerations and puncture holes. She went over his entire body, along his abdomen, down to his testicles, wrapped the cloth around the cuts on his organ, her touch light and soothing. Finished, she covered him with a fresh blanket of the sage leaves and poultices. He fell asleep under her touch, woke only when it was time for another change of dressings. It became a ritual, six times a day, and as the days drifted by, he felt his body recuperating, strength slowly beginning to infuse itself into his muscles again.

She began to sleep alongside him, being careful not to touch the tenderness of his skin until he had healed enough. She lay her soft skin against him, then pressed her face against his. It was one of the mornings when he sat up, only a few of the poultices still in place now, that she returned from outside, her face shining with the freshness of spring water. She'd put the white shirt on over a wet body and the tiny nipples pressed against the garment. He held his arms out to her and she came to him, dropped to her knees beside him. Slowly she took the blouse off, then the skirt, and he felt his breath draw in at the beauty of her, reality always better than memory.

She pushed him back onto the blanket gently but firmly and, starting with his mouth, began to press her lips gently over his entire body. He felt the sweet warmth of her mouth tracing a lambent path across his chest, her tongue flicking out over his nipples, moving down his abdomen, kissing all the healed places, moving lower, nibbling slowly down the center of his firmly muscled belly, and when she reached beyond the thick, curly nap, he was waiting for her, beckoning with man's primal invitation, the symbol of symbols. Her mouth closed around him, and he groaned with delight as he was suffused in warmth, caressed, her tongue circling, darting, playing, and he felt the tightness begin in his groin. His legs dug into the blanket and he lifted upward, unable to halt the surging explosion, reveling in the enveloping ecstasy of her lips. When he fell back onto the blanket, she lifted her head, pressed her face against him.

But he reached down, his desire still flaming, pulsating, and he turned her, came down over her, thrusting into her with the enthusiasm of the reborn, shouted with pure glee as she cried out with him, and together they hurried pleasure until the cave resounded with passion found again, ecstasy recaptured.

She slid down beside him afterward, rose on one elbow to look at him. "I'd say you're all better," she pronounced, a hint of satisfied smugness in her voice.

"That means I can get into my clothes now," Fargo said.

Her arms encircled him instantly. "Not yet," she murmured, put her head on his chest, and clung there.

But he rose later, took his extra outfit from his saddlebag, and dressed. His hand went to his hip and he smiled ruefully. "Still feel a little naked," he said. He'd get another good Colt in time. Meanwhile, he'd have to make do with the heavy Sharps rifle in the saddle holster. He saw Lisa watching him, her eyes grave.

"They're out there every day, searching," she said. "I've watched them. We've been lucky they haven't come up here."

He met the deep, waiting stare of the black liquid eyes. "You going to ask me to run again?" he said.

She shook her head. "No," she murmured.

"How come?" he asked, not hiding surprise.

"Would it do any good?" she returned.

"No," he admitted. "I've got a lot of paying back to do, not just for myself but for everyone Bart Bullmer's ever laid hands on. He's a maniac."

Lisa nodded. "Even more than I'd heard about. But how can you get to him now? He must have every hand he has out looking for us. I know he's crazy with rage that you got away," she said.

"And he won't stop, not now, not ever. He won't quit till he gets his revenge. He'll hire every gunslinger he can to find me, kill me. That's why there's no running. It'd just be buying a little time, nothing more," Fargo said.

"He's probably put two and two together by now and figured out I was the only one who could've let you out," Lisa said.

"Welcome to the club," Fargo said grimly.

"How can you possibly get to him now? It'll be even harder than before," Lisa said despairingly.

"If you can't get to the fox, you make the fox come to you."

"I don't understand," she said.

"You will. But now we sleep some. We'll do our traveling by night. It'll be safer," he told her.

"Traveling where?" she pressed.

"To get the bait," Fargo said, and she turned away, annoyed but aware she'd learn nothing more for now. She lay on the blanket and Fargo stretched his long frame beside her. It didn't take more than a few minutes before she curled up against him, and they slept until night came. He saddled the horses as Lisa put out the little fire. She climbed onto the gelding and he led the way from the cave, headed down from the high hills, south, away from Bart Bullmer's logging camp. She kept her curiosity in hand until the first pink-gray light of morning touched the trees and she saw they were at the edge of the high plains country, the relatively flatland stretched out before them.

"What are we going to do here?" she snapped out. "Or did you change your mind about running?"

"Didn't change anything," he said. "And what we're going to do first is sleep some. It's been a long night's riding and we made good time." He halted at a cool spot in the trees where the grass grew soft and thick, spread the blanket, and lay down, putting the big Sharps rifle at his side. Lisa came to him, was hard asleep against him in minutes. He slept till noon, the sun filtering through the trees, a covy of jays chattering noisily nearby. He woke Lisa, found a forest brook to wash and refill their canteens, and a cluster of apple trees served as a filling lunch.

"There's not much chance that Bullmer's boys are around here," Fargo said, edging from the trees into the open of the high plains country. "Not yet, anyway," he added.

"But there's something here," Lisa said.

Fargo nodded. "Wild horses," he said, saw her frown at him. "I'm going to rope an Ovaro," he said.

Her frown stayed. "It'll take weeks to break a wild pinto," she said.

"I'm not going to try to break him," Fargo answered. "I'm just going to rope him, bring him back, and stake him out."

Understanding began to slide across her face. "The bait," she murmured.

"You've got it," Fargo said, spurred the pinto into a fast trot. Lisa came up beside him as he scanned the land for signs of a wild herd, suddenly reined up, pointed to the hoofmarks on the ground. "Up that way," he said, sending the pinto heading for a dip in the flatland. He reached the place and looked down to where the small herd of wild horses moved across the ground, a long-maned brown stallion in the lead. Most were bays and chestnuts. There were three pintos, one a Tobiano. "No Ovaros," he said. "We move on."

"What if we don't find one?" Lisa asked as they rode on. "They're not your everyday pinto."

"We'll find one," he said with grim determination,

though he knew there was more than a little truth in her words. He found another set of tracks, followed them to where another wild herd crossed their path. This one contained a half-dozen pintos, most of them skewbalds, the rest grays and browns. A third, small herd came into sight at dusk, but it was made up mostly of solid-color mares, one dapple-gray and an Appaloosa. Fargo retired into the trees as night settled in and Lisa slept against him, tired as he.

In the morning he edged the high plains land, followed tracks up onto another stretch of land, not as rich with grass as the one below. Thin lines of serviceberry crossed the land and he'd just pushed his way through one when he reined up sharply, pointed down into a small ravinelike area below. Lisa's glance followed his arm and she saw the herd, eight wild ponies, and in the center of them, an Ovaro. She nodded as Fargo gestured for silence, started slowly down toward the herd.

The Ovaro was a good one, not as perfectly marked as his own, but good enough, Fargo noted as he slowly moved toward the herd, circling to approach downwind. His hand took the lariat that hung coiled alongside his leg, lifted the rope into position. The herd was still grazing and Fargo felt the tight smile touch his lips. It was going well. He was getting in closer than he'd hoped for, and being close was all-important. He'd have only a few precious moments when the herd caught scent of him and bolted. If the Ovaro got the jump on him, there'd be no way a horse carrying a rider could catch a wild pony in the long run. Fargo motioned for Lisa to hang back and he raised the lariat, held it ready to whirl. Just a few yards more, he muttered to himself when suddenly he saw the wild pinto's head lift, the horse's ears twitch. He saw the horse's powerful chest muscles move, the compact body start to turn. The others in the herd were alerted now, heads up, forelegs lifting to plunge into a gallop.

Fargo started to dig his heels into the pinto's sides when he saw a horse streaking toward the herd from the other side of the ravine, a bronzed, near-naked figure riding bareback on an Indian pony. "*Goddamn!*" Fargo swore as the Indian charged into the herd, one arm swinging a leather lariat over his head. The wild horses bolted, scattering, and Fargo, now galloping downhill also, saw the Indian swerve his pony after the Ovaro. The wild pony leaped forward, headed for the slope where Fargo raced down, saw him, and turned to dart away in another direction. It was all the Indian needed and he flung the lariat over the horse's neck, pulled it closed, and let his pony race along behind the Ovaro. Fargo reached the bottom of the ravine and swerved his horse after the racing Ovaro and the Indian holding on to it from his pony.

"*Son of a bitch,*" Fargo swore into the wind as the wild horse plunged on, moved up onto a stretch of flat grass, running in panic now, instinctively aware that he was no longer free, the thing around his neck dragging him, slowing his flight.

But the wild Ovaro wasn't ready to stop yet, and he continued to race across the grass, the Indian staying just behind him, hanging on to the lariat. Fargo closed distance between himself and the Indian, saw the red man look back at him. "My horse, damn your red hide," Fargo shouted in frustrated anger. The Indian, clad only in a breechclout, turned back to reining in the racing Ovaro. He was almost abreast of the wild horse now, and Fargo saw that the Ovaro was running out of steam, his strides growing markedly shorter. The Indian pulled his pony alongside the fleeing pinto, steered the wild horse toward a cluster of oaks, and Fargo saw the Ovaro slowing to a hard-breathing canter. Nearing the trees, the Indian leaped from his pony, landed lightly on both feet, and raced around a tree trunk with the end of the lariat. The Ovaro jerked to a halt, tried to rear up, but the lariat held him in. The Indian deftly secured the lariat to the tree, turned as Fargo rode up and leaped from his saddle.

The Indian took a step toward him, one hand on the handle of a tomahawk inside a leather waistband. Crow, Fargo guessed. He was tall, with the finer features of the Crow: the long, thinner nose, slightly curved; cheekbones less massive than that of most Plains tribes. He wore an armband with the diagonal lines of Crow beading on it. He was young and well-muscled, Fargo saw as he faced the bronze figure. "Dammit," he muttered. "You can get yourself any damn pony. I need that Ovaro."

He knew he was merely talking to himself, giving vent to his own desperation. The Indian didn't understand and didn't care. He had probably stalked the Ovaro for weeks. There was no way he'd give up his prize, not to anyone, above all not to a white man. That would be turning a feat of skill into an act of cowardice. It would be against honor, against everything that was important to him. Confirmation came as the Indian drew the tomahawk from his waist. Damn, Fargo swore inwardly. He knew enough Crow to make a try at communicating. He pointed to the wild horse. "Mine," he said in Crow dialect, pressed a finger into his chest with one hand. He made the sign for hunger, which also served as a sign for need. He stabbed at his chest again.

The Indian shook his head, thumped his own chest, his eyes hard as twin chips of anthracite. Dammit, Fargo swore, reached back, and drew the

133

big Sharps from the saddle holster. The red man moved toward him, the tomahawk raised. "I just need that goddamn horse," Fargo said, more to himself than to the Indian. He held the rifle in front of him as he swore again. He couldn't risk firing it. Chances were better than even that the Indian wasn't the only Crow in the vicinity. He watched the Indian's feet as the man circled and was ready when he saw the powerful toes dig into the ground. He got the rifle up as the Crow leaped, took the blow of the tomahawk against the side of the gun, and felt the rifle quiver from the force of the ax. The Indian swung the tomahawk in a short, flat arc and Fargo just got the rifle down in time to again take the thrust.

The Crow leaped, his black eyes glowing specks of coal, came in with another overhand swing, and once more Fargo used the rifle to meet the blow, but this time he countered, brought the rifle stock up in a short arc. It grazed his foe's jaw and the Indian stumbled backward, more in surprise than in pain. Fargo leaped forward, swung again with the rifle, missed as the man dived to one side. The Crow countered with another sideways swing of the tomahawk and Fargo barely managed to get the rifle up in time. The force of the blow almost sent the gun spinning from his grip and he ducked away from another swing and crashed the rifle across the Indian's chest. The man staggered back with a grunt of pain and Fargo swung the gun again, but the Crow twisted away, stumbled, regained his feet. Fargo came at him with the rifle upraised and the Indian stepped back, an expression of sudden awareness flashing in his eyes, and Fargo saw that the Indian had just realized that he didn't dare fire the rifle.

Fargo pulled back as the bronze figure came at him, swinging the tomahawk furiously. Fargo fell back, avoided two blows, took two more on the stock of the rifle, kept retreating. But the Crow felt no need for caution now and he rushed forward swinging. Fargo backpedaled, dropped to one knee, held the barrel of the rifle out as if to fire off a shot. The red man almost grinned as he leaped forward disdainfully, the tomahawk whistling through the air.

Fargo stayed on one knee but jerked his head to the side and the tomahawk grazed his ear. He thrust the rifle barrel upward with all his strength, felt it pierce the Indian's throat. The Crow gagged, staggered backward, the end of the rifle barrel still pushed into his throat. His jaw dropped open and Fargo pulled the muzzle back. A thin cascade of red spurted from the Crow's throat. He tried to gasp in air and the thin red spray spurted with greater force.

But the Crow still held his feet and Fargo saw him try to bring the tomahawk up even as he clutched at his spurting throat with his other hand. Fargo swung the heavy stock in a tremendous, upward blow. It smashed into the red man's jaw and he heard the sound of bone splintering. The Crow staggered backward again, a gargling sound coming from his throat, and his jaw hung to one side as though it didn't belong to him. Fargo rose to his feet as the Indian crumpled to the ground, twitched once, and lay still.

He let his breath out in a deep, sighing gasp, looked down at the rifle. The stock was splintered, the breech half-severed with a deep gash, the gun entirely useless. "Shit," he swore bitterly, flung the rifle a dozen yards into the air. He reached down, picked up the tomahawk, and pushed it into his belt as he saw Lisa in the distance, moving slowly toward him. She quickened her pace, reached him as he swung into the saddle.

"I was afraid to come closer," she said honestly.

"You did right to stay back," he told her.

"I was afraid it was all over," she murmured.

"It's not," he said grimly. He rode to the wild horse, and the steed blew and snorted, pawed the ground, tried to rear up again, eyes rolling back wildly. Fargo backed off a moment, let the horse calm some, then slipped his own lariat over the pinto's neck, pulled it secure, and wrapped the other end around the saddle horn. He returned to the tree, cut the Indian's lariat from the pinto, and had his own horse pull backward as the pinto instantly tried to race away.

He saw Lisa try to help, start to bring her horse around to the other side of the wild pinto and he barked sharply at her. "Keep back or he'll kick the gelding's ribs in," he said, and Lisa backed off at once. Fargo slowly shortened the lariat a few feet, wrapped it tight around his saddle horn. He moved his Ovaro sideways, a few steps at a time. The wild horse balked, rose up, and pawed the air, and Fargo let the lariat out a little, allowed the wild pinto to race in a circle. He let the horse run himself into a kind of nervous calm, carefully began to move forward, pulling him along. The wild horse balked, then ran alongside, keeping a safe distance, as though the length of the lariat made him feel free.

"He'll come along," Fargo said. "So long as we don't try to touch him, he'll come along. Instinctively he knows he's caught and he's willing to wait and see."

"For how long?" Lisa asked.

Fargo shrugged. "Long enough, if we don't push him, make him nervous." He moved alongside the trees, away from the open land, taking it very slow, halting to let the wild horse run in a circle whenever he began to grow agitated. He found a clearing in a

136

stand of timber and dismounted, tied the wild steed on a long tether, enough for him to move freely and forage on his own. "We stay here till dark," Fargo said. "Then we start back into the hills."

"And into Big Bart's backyard," Lisa said, unable to keep the fear from her voice.

Fargo sat down, pulled her to him. "I thought you understood now," he said.

"I understand, and I'm still afraid. The one doesn't cancel out the other," she said.

"I suppose not," he conceded.

Her hands clutched at him, a sudden burst of panic seizing her. "What if it goes wrong? Things do go wrong," she said.

He nodded wryly. She was right, of course. Things did go wrong, especially when they were held together by luck and lunacy. He was going to tackle a heavily armed brute of a madman with a posse of gunhands and all he had was a dead Crow's tomahawk to his name. Things definitely could go wrong. He glanced at Lisa, the black liquid eyes full of anxiousness, and he stroked her hair. "If it goes wrong, you run and you keep running," he said. Her eyes offered only reluctant agreement. "There'll be nothing to come back for this time," he said gently.

She put her head down on his chest as a patch of warm sun moved through the foliage to surround them. "One more time, Fargo? Here, now?" she murmured. "For luck?"

"For luck," he echoed as she sat up, began to unbutton the white shirt. Hell, every gambler had his own way of calling on Lady Luck for help, and he was sure as shooting being a gambler, Fargo reflected. He'd make this his way. After all, luck was a lady, wasn't she? He took one warm breast in his mouth and began a hymn to all females everywhere, past, present, and he hoped, future, young and old, sweet and savage, loving and lying. Maybe they'd always been his lucky charm, that warm, sweet, dark triangle. Hell, it was better than a rabbit's foot.

8

They rode on when night came and Fargo continued to play the wild Ovaro on a long tether, giving
him space, keeping a firm but gentle lead. It made
for slow going, but it was important to keep the wild
horse calm. But when morning slid across the sky,
they were into the hills and the towering Rocky
Mountains rose up beyond in great gray splendor.
He halted in a stand of dense-leafed oaks and dismounted. He tethered the wild horse on a long rope
that let him have the illusion of freedom and turned
back to Lisa.

"We switch horses for now," he said, and she
frowned. "Bullmer's hands will be combing these
hills soon. They'll spot an Ovaro. A distant rider on
a brown gelding won't interest them."

"Where are you going?" she asked.

"There has to be a line cabin or two in these hills.
I've got to find one," he said. "Sleep some till I get
back."

"Fat chance," she said, sniffing, brushed his cheek
with her lips. He took the gelding's reins, started to
step from the thick oaks when he halted, shrank
back into the protection of the trees. "Bullmer's boys
already?" Lisa frowned.

He shook his head, his eyes on a distant ridge

where a single file of horsemen moved like silent wraiths in and out of a line of tamaracks. "Crow, I'd guess," he said softly. "I suspect they found their friend back where I left him."

"They're looking for whoever killed him?" Lisa asked. Fargo, eyes narrowed on the distant ridge, nodded again. "But it might've been anybody, another Indian. They couldn't know why or how?" she said.

"They might have a pretty damn good idea," Fargo muttered.

"How?" Lisa frowned.

"It wouldn't be all that hard," he told her. "First, they can read signs just as well as I can, maybe better. They'd see there were two riders and a wild horse. They'd be able to follow just about exactly what happened, including the footprints that'd tell them there were only two men fighting."

"But they couldn't know the fight was over a wild Ovaro," she said.

"They could," Fargo said grimly. "That brave may have told the others he was going to catch that Ovaro. He may have been trying for weeks."

Horror flooded Lisa's eyes. "Not only Bullmer's boys but the Crow are out looking for the man on an Ovaro," she said.

"Yep, I'm getting real popular," Fargo grunted, and swung up on the gelding. "You stay in these woods. The Crow are looking east-west. They won't be this way for a while."

"Hurry back," Lisa said as he started to edge the brown gelding out of the tree cover. "God, hurry back."

Fargo sent the gelding along the hillside, crossed over a series of rises, found a narrow footpath, and carefully followed along its winding passage. A few miles on, he saw a second, steeper footpath that led

140

higher into the hills, and he guided the gelding up the tricky footing. The horse was not surefooted for all his oversize feet and Fargo wished he had his pinto under him. The path wound into evergreen country, balsam and spruce starting to appear. It leveled off but stayed well marked, and Fargo continued to follow it. He'd gone some four or so miles farther when he glimpsed the line cabin, set back a few yards from the path. He rode up to it, dismounted, and pushed the door open. It was a one-room affair, solid enough, with a single window and a crude stone hearth. Like all line cabins, it was built for shelter and not much more, a way station for those in trouble. A single overhang jutted out from one side to afford some shelter for horse or mule. But it was just what he wanted, not too close and not too far from Bart Bullmer's logging camp.

He turned the gelding and started back along the narrow footpath, his eyes taking in natural markers, a twisted tree trunk, a stunted spruce, the overhang of wild cherry where the paths joined together. The day was growing short when he crossed the hillside toward the stand of thick oaks. He had seen at least four small parties of Bullmer's men scouring the hills, waited, and watched some till they went on, circled others. But he'd seen no Crow and he was experienced enough to know that didn't mean a damn thing.

Lisa was waiting at the edge of the oaks when he rode in, bringing the gray dusk into the woods with him, and she clung to him the minute he slid out of the saddle. "I found a place to set out the bait," he told her as his eyes sought out the wild Ovaro back in the trees. "He give you any trouble?" he asked.

"A little," she said. "He got panicky twice, started to buck and rear and run in circles, got himself tangled in the rope once. I talked him quiet each time. Took me an hour the last time after I got the rope untangled."

"You did well," he said, and lowered himself to the ground. He was feeling the tiredness pull at him. It'd been twenty-four hours since he'd slept and riding a new horse was always tiring. Lisa lay down beside him and cradled his head against her. He fell asleep in minutes and she stayed holding him till he came awake in the deep of the night. She got the blanket out then and slept beside him till a few hours before dawn, when he woke. She blinked up at him.

"I'm taking the Ovaro now," he said. "I want him staked out before daybreak."

"Then what?" she asked.

"I'll come back here, leave the gelding, and go to Bullmer's on foot. I'll wait there until they take the bait. If I've figured it right, Bullmer will stay there and wait. I'll have a chance that way, just he and I," Fargo told her.

"Only he'll have a gun, maybe two," Lisa said, and her eyes flicked to the tomahawk at his waist.

Fargo's hand closed around the handle. "It'll have to do till I can get hold of something better," he said. He rose and she jumped to her feet with him, her lips pressing hard against him. Words weren't needed. He gathered the wild Ovaro, gently reeled him closer, swung onto the gelding, and secured the lariat around the saddle horn. He rode out, the stars still blinking and the moon moving too quickly toward the horizon. He crossed the hillside and the wild horse moved along behind him, and Fargo let him have as long a lead as he dared. He found the first footpath, followed it, moved carefully to spot his markers in the night. When the first edge of day broke along the high hills, he was near the line cabin, reached it as the first rays of the sun began to glint over the mountain ridges. He tied the Ovaro under the overhang at the side of the cabin, giving him enough rope so he could move out into the sunlight. He put a triple hitch on the post and went into the cabin, made a small fire, just enough to send a trickle of smoke curling up through the chimney. He packed it with damp leaves so it'd send up smoke for hours, closed the door of the cabin, stepped back, and surveyed the scene. He smiled, satisfied with what he saw; a cabin, occupied, the occupant's unsaddled Ovaro outside.

He swung onto the gelding and hurried away, riding at a gallop wherever he could as he raced the rising sun. As he neared the slope and the thick oaks where Lisa waited, he spotted one band of Bullmer's men starting into the high hills and he grunted in satisfaction. He circled, approached the forest slope from another direction. There was still no sign of the Crow, he noted as he edged into the woods and slid from the gelding.

"Done," he said simply as Lisa's deep eyes asked. She took the gelding, tethered the horse on a low branch.

"I'll be going on to Bart Bullmer's camp now," Fargo said.

"How long do I wait?" she asked gravely.

"Midnight," he said.

She made a face. "When this is over, I'll never wait again for anything," she said.

"If I'm not back, take the pinto," he told her. "It'll be something to remember me by."

"I don't need anything for that," she answered, unsmiling. She clung to him for another long moment and he finally pushed from her, turned, and began to move through the trees, falling into the long, loping stride that devoured distance and time, the rhythmic, easy lope of the wolf.

He moved out of the trees, down a steep slope, and up the next hill, slowed as he neared the top. The camp was on the other side and he could hear the sounds of voices, the clank of chains pulling logs into the chute. He dropped to one knee to scan the camp as it came into view below him. Bullmer had at least half his men out riding the hills, seeking his quarry, Fargo estimated, and his eyes grew hard as blue quartz as he spotted Bart Bullmer's huge bulk near the main house. He swore to himself as he longed to have the big Sharps in his hand. He could end it all with one shot into the overstuffed figure.

Bart Bullmer went into the house and Fargo's eyes swept the camp again. The long chute had a dozen more huge logs in it, he saw. It was almost filled with the cut trees. Rising to a crouch, he began to move down through the trees and brush, working his way closer to the campsite. The brush and tree cover extended more than halfway down the slope and he halted as it began to thin out. It was as far as he dared go in the daylight, and he lay flat, settled himself in to wait. Bullmer made a half-dozen trips in and out of the house, once to yell at three men because they'd apparently fallen behind in their quota of timber cutting. Fargo watched, listened, voices carrying easily up the slope to where he lay hidden in the brush. The sun rose into the midday sky, slowly began its journey westward, and Fargo let himself stretch, relax muscles that were easy to grow strained with waiting.

His eyes, moving back and forth across the logging camp, skimming the river at the bottom, circling, missing nothing, were the first to see the two riders racing down the slope across the river. He recognized the man in the bandanna, watched as the two horsemen forded the river opposite the long log chute. "Bart!" Ezzner shouted as he reached the nearest bank. "We got him."

Fargo peered down, his eyes narrowed as the two men leaped from their horses in front of the main house and he saw Big Bart rush out. "We got him, Bart," the man with the bandanna shouted. "He's holed up in a line cabin."

"You sure it's him?" Bullmer asked, his voice shaking with excitement.

"It's him. His Ovaro's tied up outside," the man answered. "Eddie and Ben are there now, watching the place."

"What about that bitch that let him out of here?" Bullmer roared.

"Most likely inside the cabin with him," Ezzner said.

Bullmer stepped down from his front step. "Get every man in the camp up there. Surround the place. You make sure he doesn't get away or I'll have every one of your heads," he roared.

"What if he tries to make a break for it?" Ezzner asked.

"Shoot his legs out from under him. There'll be enough of you to do that. Then bring him back here alive. I want him here alive, you hear me?" Bullmer said. "Now move, get back there."

Fargo watched the men rush off, bark orders, and he saw the others leave their work, mount up hurriedly. In minutes, Ezzner led eight riders from the camp, racing across the river at the end of the chute, obviously a shallow place. Bullmer watched them leave till they were out of sight and then edged his huge bulk back into the house.

Fargo stayed motionless as silence settled over the logging camp. The bait had been taken. It would be a spell before they realized they'd been had. He had time to let Bullmer settle down. He flexed muscles,

145

gathered inner strength. He felt his jaw grow tight, throb with the anger of vengeance. Remembered pain had suddenly flooded over him, the agony of the barbed-wire board smashing into his body, almost as real and searing as it had been that night. The throbbing pain enveloped him once again, and through it all, Bart Bullmer's roaring laughter. Fargo forced himself to hold back, fought down the urge to race down the slope with a shout of raging, avenging fury. One mistake now, one miscalculation, and justice would die with him. Bart Bullmer would survive and that couldn't be allowed to happen, no matter what the price.

Fargo's hand went to the tomahawk at his waist, drew the weapon out. He started to lift himself up when Bullmer's massive bulk sidled through the doorway. Fargo dropped flat, frowned down the slope as he saw Bullmer, a Winchester in his hands, step out from the house. Slowly Big Bart's tiny pig eyes moved in a circle around the camp, surveying the silence. He came back to the slope, let his eyes move up and down the hillside.

Fargo swore under his breath and cursed the mysterious, unexplainable power of the senses. He had seen it often enough, the sudden panic seizing the chickens when the fox drew near, a panic not made of seeing or smelling or hearing. He'd seen a groundhog lazy in the sun suddenly begin to race in darting circles long before the golden eagle swept out of the sky. An inner warning system, more developed in some than in others, but always there. Only the thoroughly civilized had lost it, laid an obliterating veneer over the purity of the senses. But the wild, the untamed, and the mad, they knew it and responded to its inner vibrations. And Big Bart was surely one of the mad.

Fargo watched as the man made another sweep of

the surroundings with his tiny pig eyes, which glittered out of the fat folds of his gross face. The sun glistened on the bald skin of his head and he wiped his palm across the round pate. Finally Bart lowered the Winchester and slid his bulk back inside the house. Fargo drew a deep breath. It was not time yet. Bullmer was too alert, too much on edge. Sadists were creatures of the senses. Fargo settled himself. There was still time. Things would go the way he'd planned for them at the little line cabin in the high hills.

He was almost right.

Smoke still curled from the stone chimney as the man with the bandanna arrived with the rest of the force. He slid from his horse, whispered to those nearest him, motioned to the others. "Get around to the back and sides," he ordered. "Surround the place but stay low."

"What if he comes out that window?" one of the others whispered.

"Blast his legs off," Ezzner said as he settled into the grass, a Henry rifle held in front of him. The cabin was silent, almost lifeless, except for the wisp of smoke that trailed up into the sky from the chimney. He was inside, though, there was no question about that, the man told himself. Probably banging that bitch with him, he grunted. He glanced at the other men. They were all flattened on the ground, rifles ready, surrounding the little cabin. They had every inch of the place covered, Ezzner grunted in satisfaction. He fidgeted with the bolt on the rifle, shifted position, shifted again, glared at the closed, silent cabin. He wasn't a man who knew how to wait. The hour that passed seemed like a day and he saw one of the others edging toward him along the ground.

"How long we gonna wait?" the man rasped.

"Till he comes out, dummy," Ezzner snapped.

"Maybe he ain't in there," the man suggested.

"Of course he's in there. There's his Ovaro and the chimney's smoking," Ezzner hissed.

"Not anymore it ain't," the man returned. "It stopped ten minutes ago." Ezzner stared up at the rooftop. Smoke had indeed stopped drifting from the chimney.

"So it stopped," he said. "Get back in place. He's in there."

The man crawled away and Ezzner stared at the cabin, suddenly feeling uneasy. Maybe the bastard had spotted them and was holding back, waiting for a chance to make a break for it. Ezzner's mouth tightened. Maybe the bastard was going to wait for dark and then try to run for it. Son of a bitch, Ezzner cursed. He wasn't going to wait around for him to try that. Maybe lose the bastard and have to face Bart Bullmer. He motioned to the man nearest him, whispered hoarsely. "Move in a few feet closer. Pass the word along," he said. He crawled forward with the others, halted, stared at the silent cabin. He glanced at the sky, saw the sun heading toward one corner. He spat, crawled to position himself behind a low rock. He'd waited all he was going to wait. The bastard would come out or they'd go in and get him, even if it meant losing a half-dozen hands. He raised his voice, shouted to the cabin.

"Come on out," he called. "You're covered on all sides." He waited, but there was no answer from inside the cabin. "You ain't got a chance. Come on out with your hands up," he tried. Silence was his only reply. He glared at the closed door. His uneasiness was growing into alarm. He put the rifle to his shoulder. "Get the hell out here or we'll blast you out," he

yelled. Once again there was no reply, no movement, not even a sound from inside the cabin.

He called to the men nearest him. "Blast a few
rounds into that goddamn cabin," he ordered. Rifle
fire erupted at once, a volley of sound that echoed
through the high hills. He held up a hand and the
firing halted. There was still no answer from inside
the cabin. Ezzner felt the perspiration suddenly
coating his brow. "Give him another round," he ordered, and once more the hills resounded to the
shots. Ezzner watched as the door slowly swung
open, the crude wooden latch shot away. The door
half-fell from its lone hinge and he could see inside
the cabin—or most of it—and what he could see was
empty.

"Shit," he swore, pulled himself to a crouch. "Rush
him," he yelled at the others, catapulted forward a
few steps behind the others. Some ran firing, others
just raced toward the cabin. Ezzner reached the
door as two of the others halted there and he
pushed them aside. The cabin was empty, not a living soul in it. "Son of a bitch," Ezzner cursed.

"Where is he?" one of the others asked.

Ezzner aimed a backhand blow at the man, who
ducked away. "How the hell do I know?" Ezzner
shouted in rage. "Maybe he saw us and he's outside
someplace, hiding somewhere." Ezzner spun on his
heel, still cursing, stalked out of the cabin, his eyes
sweeping the hills. "We'll comb every inch of this
place, he said. "If he's out there, he's not too damn
far away." The man's eyes came to rest on the
Ovaro. "Wherever he is, he's goin' to have to walk,
because I'm taking that goddamn fancy pinto," he
growled. As the others started for their horses,
Ezzner strode to the pinto, pulled the horse toward
him by its tether. The horse snorted, started to rear
up, but Ezzner leaped on its back.

The Ovaro froze for a moment at the new sensa-
tion, gathered its deep-chested power, and flung itself into the air, hind legs kicking out almost
vertically. Ezzner sailed from its back. He was still
in midair when the arrow went into his chest. He hit
the ground facedown and drove the arrow out
through his back.

Fargo decided not to inch his way down. He rose
on cat's feet, raced down the slope to the rear of the
main house, ducked low beneath the windows,
reached the front, and dropped to one knee. He
heard Bart Bullmer inside, his huge bulk moving to
the door, and he waited, his head around the edge
of the house, the tomahawk in his hand. Bullmer
stepped out carefully, the Winchester in his arms,
his brow finding space for a frown. Fargo held his
position, saw Bullmer turn, see him, and surprise
widened the tiny pig eyes. The man blasted a shot
off, but Fargo had ducked back. He ran to the rear
corner, slipped behind it, poked his head out, and
drew another shot from the rifle. This one singed his
hair as he pulled back.

He heard the click of an empty barrel and his lips
pulled back in satisfaction as he leaped forward, the
tomahawk in his hand. Bullmer turned to meet him,
slowly backed as Fargo came toward him. He took
the rifle by the barrel to use as a club and waited. A
cold, beckoning grin oozed out from the folds of fat
in the huge head. "Come on," Bullmer growled. "I'm
gonna enjoy this." He took a step backward, stopped
at the edge of the row of flat stones that made a
crude terrace in front of the house.

Fargo moved forward, lifted onto the balls of his
feet, weaved, feinted with the tomahawk. Bullmer
refused to be drawn in. He raised the rifle as though
it were a toy bat, waited. Fargo moved in closer,

feinted again, but this time he swung the tomahawk in a short, flat sideways arc. It hit the huge figure high on the side of the ribs and Fargo felt the stone blade cleave into the rolls of fat, come to a halt. Blood spurted from Bart Bullmer's side, but Fargo knew the blow hadn't struck deep enough to do real damage. He ducked down as he saw the stock of the rifle coming at his head in a tremendous swing. He'd expected the counterblow, was ready for it, and the rifle passed over his head. He hadn't expected Bullmer to hurl himself forward after the rifle and the three hundred pounds slammed into him like a runaway mule team.

He felt himself sprawling backward onto the stones, kept his hold on the tomahawk. But he'd no time for a blow. Bullmer was bringing the rifle down with both hands to crash his skull. Fargo rolled, kept rolling, saw the rifle hit the stones and smash in two. He got to his feet, rushed at the big bulk, and brought the tomahawk around in a short, flat blow. Bullmer, quick for all his bulk, pulled his body to the side and the tomahawk only sliced through the fat fleshy fold protecting his shoulder blade. The swing brought Fargo around, off balance and he saw the treelike arm coming at him as Bullmer swung a backward blow. He tried to drop, but the arm crashed into the top of his head, not hard enough to stun but with enough force to send him sprawling backward into the dirt. He scrambled to his feet, got the tomahawk up, but Bullmer wasn't following through. Instead, the big man leaped to the side, and too late, Fargo saw the long-handled lumberjack's ax leaning against a pile of firewood.

Bart Bullmer seized the weapon with a roar, turned, came at the big black-haired man. A thin line of spit trailed from his thick lips and blood ran down his left side and spattered from the sliced flesh

151

of his back. He raised his thick arms and swung the ax as if it were a plaything, advancing as though he were a prehistoric caveman. The heavy ax whistled through the air and Fargo fell backward, caught himself, ducked, and continued to pull back. He tried to duck under one whistling swing of the ax, to get in close enough to use the tomahawk, and he just avoided having his head split in two as Bullmer swung the ax backhanded. Fargo twisted away, backed, almost tripped over a piece of wood. He had to make a move, and fast, he realized. He couldn't avoid the blow forever. Another stumble, a split-second error, a simple mistake, and the ax would splinter him as though he were dry wood. He leaped away, put distance between himself and Bullmer's furious swings.

He half crouched, raised the tomahawk, grimaced as he did so. He'd be throwing away his only weapon, but he had no choice and he was grateful for one thing. He couldn't miss Bart Bullmer. The big man continued to come at him, the heavy ax poised. Fargo took a step backward and sent the tomahawk through the air. Bullmer twisted his huge body, raised one giant arm, and Fargo saw the tomahawk bury itself in a thick roll of fat just below the man's armpit. He heard Bullmer grunt, stagger sideways for a step. The tomahawk hung there as if embedded in a barrel of hog fat. Bullmer set the ax down, reached around with his other hand, and pulled the tomahawk out. A stream of blood poured down his side at once, but Bullmer ignored it. He paused to throw the tomahawk fifty yards away into the brush, picked up the ax, and started toward Fargo, a twisted smile on his thick lips.

Fargo moved backward in a half-circle, staying away from the advancing giant, and his eyes swept the camp. They paused on a stout length of two-by-four, but he discarded the thought. Bullmer would cut it in two with the ax. He saw Bullmer quickening his steps, his wounds pouring out blood but doing little else to slow him. Fargo moved backward again, realized that Bullmer was closing the space between them. He was being backed into the side of the log chute and he started to dive to the side when, instead of swinging the ax, Bullmer flung it sideways. Fargo saw it hurtling at him, tried to duck away, but the handle smashed into his temple. He felt himself go down on one knee as the world spun away. He shook his head and the world righted itself but not in time for him to avoid the kick that smashed into his side.

He felt himself being lifted into the air by the force of the blow as his side exploded in pain. When he hit the ground, he tried to roll, felt Bullmer's hands grab for him and miss. He got to one knee as the huge face loomed in front of him and he saw thick-fingered hands reach for his throat. He brought up a tremendous uppercut, smashed it into Bullmer's chin. The huge face jerked backward for a moment and Fargo got to his feet, knew it was useless to hit at the thick body, and smashed another blow into Bullmer's face. He saw the folds of fat shake and a line of red oozed out from between the folds. Bullmer's roar of pain and rage filled the air, and Fargo saw the heavy arm smashing down at him. He tried to parry the blow, but the treelike arm drove through his defense and Fargo's head spun again as he fell. His eyes glazed and he felt the dirt stabbing into his face, shook his head to clear it, and saw Bart Bullmer's hands closing around his neck. He drove his own hands upward, broke the man's grip before he had it closed, but Bullmer's arms were around him, lifting him, flinging him into the air.

Fargo felt his body shudder, a flame of pain shoot through him as he hit against something hard, dropped to the ground. On all fours, he saw the side of the log chute, glimpsed the giant shadow on the ground beside him. He tried to dive to the side, but the kick still grazed his ribs and he felt his breath stop. He landed against the side of the log chute again, a curtain of grayness descending over him. He rolled away, stones catching him in the face, and the sharp pain tore aside the gray curtain. He rolled onto his back, saw Bart Bullmer towering over him. The man had the ax in his hands again, and in horror Fargo saw him start to raise it high in the air.

He half-rolled, half-dived, used his arms to pull himself along the ground. His hand closed on something cold, hard metal, and he focused on the object, saw the length of heavy chain lying on the ground, six, maybe seven feet of it. Bullmer moved stiff-legged after him, the ax held high, determined to end it with one bone-crushing blow. Fargo flung himself onto his back, called on a last reservoir of strength somewhere inside his body, desperation and will infusing muscle and sinew. He sent the heavy chain lashing upward, watched it curl around Bullmer's forearm. He pulled, and the huge form fell forward, the ax dropping from the man's hands. Bullmer landed on his hands and knees almost beside him and Fargo pulled the chain free. Bullmer started to rise and Fargo sent the heavy chain lashing out again. This time it curled around the giant form's beefy neck like a metal snake.

Bullmer fell backward, started to claw at the chain that encircled his neck, but Fargo slammed his foot onto one end of the chain, driving it into the ground. He seized the other end with both hands, pulled upward, straining the last ounce of strength in back and leg muscles. He looked down at Bart

154

Bullmer as the heavy chain tightened around his neck. The folds of the huge face shook and spittle oozed from the thick lips. His hands tried to pull at the chain, but his fingers slipped from the smoothness of the metal links. Fargo took a half-hitch in the chain and continued to pull. Bart Bullmer's arms dropped to his sides, flopped helplessly, making him look like a vulture with a broken wing.

Fargo watched as the huge face seemed to grow gray and the tiny pig eyes became almost invisible points. He continued pulling on the chain in his hands until the folds of fat that made up Bart Bullmer's face stopped shaking. He stepped back, forced his hands to open, and the end of the chain slid to the ground. Bart Bullmer's bald head fell to one side like a huge grapefruit rolling off a plate. It was over. Fargo repeated the words to himself as he sank to the ground, every ounce of his strength drained. He fell against the side of the log chute on his knees, listened to the harsh sound of his own breathing. It was a welcome sound, nonetheless. He moved an arm and it was as though he were moving a lead weight.

He blinked, felt the frown digging into his forehead. He heard something else over the sound of his harsh breathing. Shouts, hoofbeats. Painfully he pulled himself to his feet, using the side of the log chute for support, blinked again, focused on the riders racing down the slope across the river. Bullmer's men, riding with desperate speed, pushing their horses. He shook his head, pulled his head back. They weren't supposed to be back yet, not yet. He'd nothing left to stand up to them. Damn, it wasn't supposed to end this way. He'd won only to lose.

He lowered his head, stared at the riders as they reached the opposite bank and started to ford the river. They were crossing at their usual place, opposite end of the log chute. Fargo flung a desperate glance at the ground. The long-handled woodsman's ax was only a few steps away. He took a step toward it, almost fell, held himself steady, got his hands on the ax, and pulled it to him. He raised it, felt it waver as he barely had strength enough to hold it aloft, brought it crashing down on the wooden bolt holding one end of the log chute closed. The bolt sheared off and the one end of the chute gate fell open. It was enough. The tremendous pressure of the logs tore open the bolt at the other side and Fargo dropped to his knees as the giant logs cascaded from the chute with the roar of a hundred cannon.

Fargo saw the riders just reach the near bank, look in horror at the huge logs hurtling at them. Some tried to turn their horses, others dived to the ground, and a few were thrown as their mounts bolted. It made little difference as the mass of logs, traveling at breakneck speed in moments, slammed into them. Fargo heard a few muffled screams, shouts broken off in midair as he sank to the ground, lay there half-conscious, his body shaking with strain and exhaustion. Dimly he heard the roar of the logs cease and silence take over the camp once again. He lay still, gathered energy back slowly until finally he pulled himself up, his muscles still weak but at least able to respond. His eyes swept the scene before him.

A few logs clung together in the river as the rest slowly drifted away. He moved toward the riverbank, past a litter of broken bodies. A six-gun lay on the ground, an old Walker. He picked it up. It was better than nothing. Fargo caught a glimpse of movement out of the corner of his eye, raised the gun, and whirled. A figure lay on the ground, an ugly bruise across his temple. "Don't shoot, mister," the man pleaded. "I ain't even got a gun."

Fargo lowered the pistol, stepped to where the man lay. "How come you got back so fast?" he asked.

"Raced all the way. Wanted to keep our scalps," the man said. Fargo waited and he drew a deep breath. "They hit us just when we found the line cabin was empty. They got half the boys in their first round and the rest of us took off. Ezzner took the first arrow right through his chest when he jumped onto that fancy pinto."

Fargo almost smiled. But it hurt too much. He turned, walked slowly away, headed up to the slope. He didn't bother to glance at the still, huge lump that lay on the ground with the heavy chain necklace. The dusk was beginning to soften the land as he painfully made his way up the slope, pausing to rest every few yards. He'd just reached the treeline when he saw the figure coming toward him, long jet hair trailing. Behind her, he saw the horses and he met the deep black eyes as she searched his face, read the drained exhaustion in it.

"You were supposed to wait back in the oaks," he muttered.

"That was your idea," she said.

He nodded, brushed past her, and climbed slowly into the saddle, stroked the gleaming black neck of the Ovaro. She watched him, her eyes studying him.

"Where to?" she asked.

"You tell me," he said.

"Wherever you're going," she answered instantly.

"Try again," he said.

"I've a distant aunt in the Dakota territory, a place called Coopersville."

"I'll get you to the territory border. There's a stage that goes back to the Dakotas. Runs once a

157

week and it'll take us a good while to get there," he told her.

"It will indeed," she said softly, and Fargo smiled as he wheeled the pinto around.

Lisa made good on her word. It took them a very good while to reach the stage depot on the territory border, but the day came when she paused at the stagecoach door, her black eyes on the big man with the lake-blue eyes. "I was wrong, thinking I could convince you to change your mind." She half-smiled.

"Can't," he said. "But you came closer than most."

She studied the intense, handsome face. "I'll be remembering that," she said, smiled reflectively. "Maybe there'll be another time and another place."

"Maybe," he allowed, watched her turn and enter the dust-laden stage. He swung gracefully into the saddle. Other times and other places still had to wait for promises still to be kept. He wheeled the horse away, the man on the Ovaro, the Trailsman.

LOOKING FORWARD!

The following is the opening section
from the next novel in the exciting
Trailsman series from Signet:

The Trailsman #12:
CONDOR PASS

*1861—a land called Arizona,
south of Diablo Canyon.*

"You just naturally say damnfool things, honey, or
have you been working at it?" Fargo asked the
young woman.

"Neither, thank you," she said stiffly.

He studied her for a moment. Bitterness robbed
her face of some of its beauty, giving her an edge of
hardness. But she was still uncommonly attractive,
dark-brown hair curled in front, straight where it
fell to her shoulders, a thin nose, nice lines to her
face, and well-formed lips. Tall, she had good,
square shoulders and enough of breast to push the
neckline of the maroon dress outward in a full,
smooth rise. But it was her eyes that held him, seawater eyes, blue green that shifted with her every
change in emotion. They'd turned to an ice blue
now.

"Do you remember what people said about it?" she
asked.

Fargo nodded. It hadn't been more than a month
back. "Hard words, mostly," he said.

"They said it was bound to end bad," she pressed.

"That, and more," he answered. "Some said fools deserve whatever happens to them. Others said that when you go into a grizzly's cave you're just naturally asking to be killed, and then some just called it a terrible thing and didn't want any talking or thinking about it."

"A good hiding place, that," the young woman said, and the bitterness drew her lips tight.

"But nobody called it murder," Fargo commented. "Until now."

Her seawater eyes shifted into blue green again, but they held steady, taking nothing back. "And that makes me a damnfool, is that it?" she said stiffly.

"Pretty much so, honey," he said.

"I believe I told you the name is Athena," she said, and he shrugged away the reprimand in her tone. "Well, I'm not a damnfool and I think you could hear me out," she speared.

He nodded. Her letter had promised him expenses just to meet with her outside Drovers Bend. "Guess that's only fair," he conceded.

"Please sit down. I have something to show you. It'll take me a moment to get it," she said. He watched her turn crisply, start into an adjoining room. The maroon dress hung nicely over a round rear, swayed rhythmically as she walked, a nice steady stride. Fargo eased his big powerful frame into a small chair, a frown clinging to his forehead. He heard her snap open a suitcase and rummage through it, and the frown continued to stay with him, his lake-blue eyes narrowing in thought. Her letter, which had reached him at General Delivery in Elbow Creek, had been signed only Miss Athena. But her offer for his talents, plus expenses, just to meet with her had been more than inviting enough to bring him here. She'd wasted no time on small talk when he arrived.

"The Condor Pass massacre, you've heard about it, of course," she'd thrown at him.

He'd nodded. There weren't many who hadn't heard of it, an attack that made people shudder in horror in a land where horror was as common as chickweed along a roadside. Six wagons and an escort of outriders, twenty people in all, and there'd been only one known survivor. Even without his words, the grim evidence had turned the stomachs of strong men. Fargo remembered how, when he'd first heard about it, he'd thought it an unusually brutal attack even for the Comanche. But in this dry and harsh place the Indians had named Arizona, the unusual was usual.

The sun had been a little less burning that Sabbath morning when the six wagons slowly rolled into Condor Pass, all big-wheeled Conestogas with reinforced spring and weighted undercarriages. They had halted in the very center of the high rock pass for Sabbath services and everyone had gathered in a loose circle around the Reverend Eli Clairborne, an ordained Methodist minister, and his wife, Letitia, who led the hymn singing.

The Anderson family—George, Martha, and their ten-year-old son, Josh—along with Henry Corn and his two daughters, Amy and Beth, were seated in the front of the circle, the adults forming a ring behind them. Reverend Eli Clairborne was a hell-fire-and-brimstone preacher, delivering the words of the Good Book with impassioned tones and rolling cadences. The very rocks of Condor Pass rang out with the sounds of Biblical prophecy. He'd chosen a passage out of Genesis for this Sabbath morning and in between the words "trespassers" and "forgiveness," the arrow struck him full in the mouth, traveling in a downward arc. It went all the way through his mouth and halted deep in the back of his throat. The reverend fell with the arrow sticking out of his mouth as though he were sucking on a giant, feathered candystick.

Someone screamed, only once. The confines of Condor Pass exploded in flying arrows and the sound of gunfire. The Comanche came from all sides, leaping down from the rock crevices, sliding over the tops of stones. A follow-up party charged in on horseback. Those trapped in the pass had little chance. Many never got to fire off a single shot in return and they were killed instantly. They were the lucky ones. A good number were taken alive. They had hoped that surrender might keep them alive. It was an empty hope.

The escort outriders were taken first as the Comanche rounded up their captives. The men were separated from the women, hands bound behind their backs with leather thongs so they could watch helplessly as the women were stripped, then raped, each one at least a half-dozen times. Only the two young girls, Amy and Beth Corn, were held aside and not touched. But they were forced to witness, and that would be seared inside them for the rest of their lives, visions no one could ever erase from their souls. After the Comanche had pleasured themselves enough with the women, they turned to another pleasure—torture. Some women were hung from an old dead tree by their hair until they passed out from the pain. Others had bear claws driven through their nipples, and Letitia Clairborne, the oldest woman in the group, was held with her legs spread-eagled while arrows were shot into her crotch until she resembled a deformed porcupine.

The men were dragged behind horses, whipped until their skins hung in shreds, and while still alive, their penises cut off. Little Josh Anderson was merely slammed into a rock until his small head split open.

Only one man survived, Charlie Sims, grayed and grizzled, the cook hired for the expedition. He had not been part of the circle of worshipers listening to the Sabbath-morning sermon, a fact that later only fortified his lifelong distrust of religion. When the attack came, he dived into a narrow crevice, unseen and unnoticed. He was also the only man who, from the depths of the crevice, had a chance to see the Comanche leader who looked down from the top of a tall rock. But Charlie Sims crawled back into the crevice, as far as he could go, turned his face to the stone walls. He stayed there after the Comanche had gone, his head so ringing with the screams of pain and terror that he thought the attack was still going on twenty-four hours after it had ended.

When he finally crawled from his hiding place, the sight that met his eyes made him too sick to run for another half a day. But he eventually gathered himself and retraced the paths he had come on in the wagons, hiding as much as running, and the horror he had left behind haunted his every step. Finally, three days later, he met up with a team of prospectors who took him to a way-station town called Dry Patch. There he told his story to a traveling U.S. marshal. In time, a heavily armed burial party was sent out. They returned with shock in their eyes and confirmed that nothing old Charlie Sims had said had been an exaggeration.

Such was the massacre at Condor Pass.

Fargo clicked his thoughts off, but the same overwhelming reaction came to him again, as it had that first time he'd heard the terrible story. It seemed too vicious even for the Comanche. Yet some would argue that there was nothing too vicious for the Comanche, and perhaps they were right. The U.S. government had bought Arizona from the Mexicans, but the red man had never recognized the rights of either seller or buyer. The Comanche, Navaho, Apache, Jicarilla and Mescalero claimed this land, and of them all, the Comanche demanded the highest price of those who trespassed. It was the Indian who had named this harsh, dry land where water came only in small doses, Arizona, "the place of little springs." Perhaps Condor Pass had been only one more warning by the Comanche, Fargo wondered, a message that the nature of hate was growing more fearful.

He glanced up as the young woman came back into the room, a piece of paper in her hand. "This is part of a letter written before the wagon train left Drovers Bend," she said. "Please read the last paragraph."

Fargo took the letter from her, noted that it was the second page of a long missive. No scrawled, crude handwriting, he saw, but a fine, cursive penmanship, the script of an educated person. "Who wrote this?" he asked.

The young woman paused for a moment. "Is that important?" she said in annoyance.

His lake-blue eyes narrowed on her. "Don't play games with me, honey," he growled.

"Athena," she snapped, the seawater eyes turning a dark blue. "The letter was written by Professor Raymond Neils, one of the people on the expedition."

Fargo's brows lifted. "Professor?"

"He was an anthropologist specializing in Indian culture," she answered.

"Indian culture," Fargo grunted. "He saw some of it, didn't he?"

The young woman's lips thinned into a straight line. "The last paragraph," she said.

Fargo lowered his eyes to the few lines at the bottom of the page.

> While I fully expect to return, I am uneasy about some things in this expedition. There are no extra horses being taken along and I heard the cook, a Mr. Sims, complain that not enough essential provisions were being stocked for a trip as lengthy as this is destined to be. But then I may just be suffering the pangs of nervousness as well as excitement, for it is dangerous country into which we are moving.

The paragraph ended and Fargo handed the letter back. The young woman peered at his strong-planed, intense, handsome face for some sign, found none, and finally threw the question at him. "Doesn't that seem strange to you?" she asked.

"A little unusual," Fargo admitted. "But maybe the wagonmaster figured to pick up horses and supplies somewhere along the way."

"Nonsense. No wagon train counts on that and you know it," she snapped.

"Maybe so, but that still doesn't come out to what you're saying," he answered.

"It's part of it. No extra supplies or horses were taken because somebody knew they'd never make it beyond Condor Pass," she said. "And I've more that adds up to the same thing."

"You know how crazy that sounds?" Fargo asked.

"I know, but I'll stick to it. Condor Pass was planned to happen and that makes it murder, pure and simple," she said.

"Why? You have a reason?" Fargo pushed at her.

The seawater eyes shifted to a blue gray, and he saw her smooth jaw tighten. "No, I don't have that yet, but I'll find it," she said tersely.

Fargo drew a sigh. "You didn't send for me to come all this way out here just to test out a lot of theories," Fargo commented.

"That's right," she agreed. "I want to hire you to help me prove what I'm saying."

"Prove?" Fargo almost winced. "How in hell do you figure to do that?"

"I'm going to do it all over again. I'm going to take another wagon train through Condor Pass," she said with a tone of triumph.

Fargo felt the frown digging into his brow as he stared at her. "I take back what I said about your being a damnfool. You're a plain, dyed-in-the-wool crazy," he said.

Wild Westerns From SIGNET

☐ **RUFF JUSTICE #1: SUDDEN THUNDER by Warren T. Long-tree.** (#AE1028—$2.50)*

☐ **RUFF JUSTICE #2: NIGHT OF THE APACHE by Warren T. Longtree.** (#AE1029—$2.50)*

☐ **RUFF JUSTICE #3: BLOOD ON THE MOON by Warren T. Longtree.** (#AE1215—$2.50)*

☐ **RUFF JUSTICE #4: WIDOW CREEK by Warren T. Longtree.** (#AE1422—$2.50)*

☐ **THE TRAILSMAN #1: SEVEN WAGONS WEST by Jon Sharpe.** (#AE1052—$2.25)

☐ **THE TRAILSMAN #2: THE HANGING TRAIL by Jon Sharpe.** (#AE1053—$2.25)

☐ **THE TRAILSMAN #3: MOUNTAIN MAN KILL by Jon Sharpe.** (#AE1130—$2.25)

☐ **THE TRAILSMAN #4: THE SUNDOWN SEARCHERS by Jon Sharpe.** (#AE1158—$2.25)

☐ **THE TRAILSMAN #5: THE RIVER RAIDERS by Jon Sharpe.** (#AE1199—$2.25)

☐ **THE TRAILSMAN #6: DAKOTA WILD by Jon Sharpe.** (#E9777—$2.25)

☐ **THE TRAILSMAN #7: WOLF COUNTRY by Jon Sharpe.** (#E9905—$2.25)

☐ **THE TRAILSMAN #8: SIX-GUN DRIVE by Jon Sharpe.** (#AE1024—$2.25)

*Price slightly higher in Canada

**Buy them at your local
bookstore or use coupon
on next page for ordering.**

𝄞

SIGNET Double Westerns For Your Library

- ☐ **BRANDON'S POSSE** and **THE HELL MERCHANT** by Ray Hogan. (#J8857—$1.95)
- ☐ **APACHE HOSTAGE** and **LAW OF THE GUN** by Lewis B. Patten. (#J9420—$1.95)
- ☐ **THE DEVIL'S GUNHAND** and **THE GUNS OF STRINGAREE** by Ray Hogan. (#J9355—$1.95)
- ☐ **FIGHTING MAN** and **THE MARSHAL** by Frank Gruber. (#J9125—$1.95)
- ☐ **LAWMAN FOR SLAUGHTER VALLEY** and **PASSAGE TO DODGE CITY** by Ray Hogan. (#J9173—$1.95)
- ☐ **PATCHSADDLE DRIVE** and **SHOOTOUT AT SIOUX WELLS** by Cliff Farrell. (#J9258—$1.95)
- ☐ **RIM OF THE DESERT** and **DEAD MAN'S RANGE** by Ernest Haycox. (#J9210—$1.95)
- ☐ **SADDLE & RIDE** and **THE FEUDISTS** by Lewis B. Patten. (#J9467—$1.95)
- ☐ **SMOKE OF THE GUN** and **WILD RIDERS** by John S. Daniels and Lee Hoffman. (#J8667—$1.95)
- ☐ **WAR PARTY** and **THE CROSSING** by John S. Daniels. (#J8761—$1.95)

Buy them at your local bookstore or use this convenient coupon for ordering.

THE NEW AMERICAN LIBRARY, INC.,
P.O. Box 999, Bergenfield, New Jersey 07621

Please send me the books I have checked above. I am enclosing $_____
(please add $1.00 to this order to cover postage and handling). Send check or money order—no cash or C.O.D.'s. Prices and numbers are subject to change without notice.

Name_____

Address_____

City _____ State _____ Zip Code _____
Allow 4-6 weeks for delivery.
This offer is subject to withdrawal without notice.